TOP COW PRODUCTIONS PRESENTS

Created by

LINDA SEJIC, MATT HAWKINS & JENNI CHEUNG

Published by Top Cow Productions, Inc.
Los Angeles

Top Cow Productions Presents...

VOLUME THREE

CREATED BY
Linda Sejic, Matt Hawkins and Jenni Cheung

WRITTEN BY
Matt Hawkins

ART BY
Yishan Li

LETTERING BY
Troy Peteri

BASED ON A STORY AND CHARACTERS DEVELOPED BY
Linda Sejic
Stjepan Sejic
Matt Hawkins
Jenni Cheung

DEDICATED TO MARK AND CARRIE

SWING, VOL. 3. First printing. November 2020. Published by Image Comics, Inc. Offic of publication: 2701 NW Vaughn St., Suite 780, Portland, OR 97210.

ISBN: 978-1-5343-1610-2. For international rights, contact: matt@topcow.con

CAST

Cathy Chang

Dan Lincoln

Blake Lincoln

Ashley Lincoln

Mom

In the last two volumes of
Swing
DAN LINCOLN WAS A BRIGHT YOUNG GRAD STUDENT AND A GIFTED WRITER...
DETERMINED TO CRAFT THE NEXT GREAT AMERICAN NOVEL.
CATHY CHANG WAS A COLLEGE FRESHMAN, ON HER OWN AND CUTTING LOOSE FOR THE FIRST TIME IN HER SHELTERED LIFE.
WHEN THEY FIRST MET, SPARKS FLEW.
IT WASN'T LONG BEFORE THEIR "TUTORING SESSIONS" TURNED INTO SOMETHING ELSE...
AND WHEN THEIR FLING TURNED INTO SOMETHING DEEPER...
PREGNANT
NOT PREGNANT
THEY FOUND THEMSELVES FACING A NEW CHALLENGE - TOGETHER.
BUT FOR ALL THE FEAR THAT COMES WITH A SHOT-GUN WEDDING, DAN AND CATHY WERE HAPPY.
THEY BELIEVED IN EACH OTHER. WHAT-EVER CAME NEXT...
THEY COULD FACE IT TOGETHER.

BUT 8 YEARS AND TWO KIDS LATER, THE MAGIC STARTED TO FADE.
ROUTINE REPLACED ROMANCE.
RESPONSIBILITY
DAN STARTED TEACHING HIGH SCHOOL ENGLISH --
AND SPENT MORE TIME GRINDING AWAY AT RPGS THAN WRITING HIS NOVEL.
CATHY ENDED UP IN THE ENTERTAINMENT INDUSTRY --
COURTING CLIENTS AND MANAGING A TEAM OF WEB DESIGNERS AND ENGINEERS.
THE MORE THEY DRIFTED, THE MORE TEMPTATION LOOMED.
BUT THEY LOVED EACH OTHER.
THEY DIDN'T WANT TO FEEL THIS RESENTMENT.
THEY BOTH WANTED TO FEEL CLOSER...
THEY WANTED TO FEEL THE HEAT AGAIN.
AND CATHY HAD A PLAN TO PUT THE SPICE BACK INTO THEIR MARRIAGE.
THEY WOULD BECOME SWINGERS.
I THINK I'D LIKE TO TRY THAT.

THEY MADE RULES. THEY RE-SPECTED EACH OTHER'S BOUND-ARIES.
AND AT FIRST, MERELY ENTER-TAINING THE IDEA SEEMED TO BRING BACK THE OLD EXCITE-MENT.
WHAT THE FUCK?
BUT DAN WAS SKEPTICAL AND INSECURE.
CATHY WAS PATIENT...
BUT SHE WORRIED THEIR MAR-RIAGE WAS ENDING BEFORE THEY COULD EVEN TRY OPENING IT UP.
SHE CONFIDED IN AN OLD FRIEND...
SO WITH DEBBIE'S HELP, CATHY HATCHED A PLAN.
NO STRANGERS, NO SPECIAL CLUBS --
JUST GOOD OLD FASHIONED SEDUCTION.
IT WAS FAR FROM TRADITIONAL, BUT IT WORKED.
HERE WAS SOMETHING NEW, AND DAN AND CATHY LOVED IT.
AND LOVED EACH OTHER MORE FOR IT.

AFTER CATHY GOT DAN A SERIES OF THREESOMES WITH HER FRIENDS, HE WAS WILLING TO TRY A FOURSOME WITH ANOTHER COUPLE.
HI, GUYS. I'M MARY AND THIS IS MY HUSBAND CLINT. WE USE CHERI AND JACK UNTIL WE SEE THE COUPLE'S LEGIT.
FIGHTING THROUGH A SERIES OF FAKES AND FLAKES VIA THE SWINGERS' ONLINE DATING SITES THEY FINALLY MET CLINT AND MARY, A COUPLE THEY BOTH LIKED AND THEY HAVE THEIR FIRST SUCCESSFUL COUPLES SWING.
DAN AND CATHY GET MORE EXPERIENCE AND DAN LEARNS THAT HE MIGHT NEED VIAGRA FROM TIME TO TIME TO MAINTAIN HIS ERECTION BECAUSE OF THE ANXIETY IN THESE SITUATIONS.
ARE YOU OKAY? YOU'RE STILL NOT HARD.
NOT AT ALL. IT'S JUST A REGULAR FRIDAY, BUT I WANTED TO TREAT YOU TO A SPECIAL NIGHT OUT.
WANTING TO MAKE SURE THEIR RELATIONSHIP STAYED ROCK SOLID, THEY INSTITUTED REGULAR DATE NIGHTS FOR JUST THE TWO OF THEM.
THEIR COMMUNICATION, HONESTY AND SHARED EXPERIENCE RESULTED IN A RENAISSANCE IN THEIR RELATIONSHIP. LIFE WAS GOOD.

WITH HIS RELATIONSHIP IN A GREAT PLACE AND INSPIRED BY THEIR NEW LIFESTYLE, DAN FOCUSES MORE ON TRYING TO RESTART HIS WRITING CAREER.
I'M CATHY CHANG, MANY OF YOU KNOW ME ALREADY. FOR THE PAST FIVE YEARS WE'VE DONE A SERIES OF TRAILERS FOR YOUR FILMS.
SINCE YOU'RE IN THE FILM BUSINESS, I THOUGHT IT APPROPRIATE MY TEAM PUT TOGETHER A SHORT FILM TO SHOW WHAT I'M PITCHING, RATHER THAN JUST TALKING AT YOU.
CATHY WAS ALSO ADVANCING WELL IN HER CAREER AND PITCHED AN OVERALL DEAL TO A MAJOR STUDIO.
ONE OF DAN'S PRIMARY CONCERNS ABOUT THIS LIFESTYLE WAS IT CROSSING OVER INTO THEIR REAL LIVES. HE WANTED TO KEEP THIS PART OF THEM COMPARTMENTALIZED AND SEPARATE FROM EVERYTHING ELSE. SO IT CREATED A PROBLEM FOR CATHY WHEN SHE RAN INTO CLINT DURING ONE OF HER STUDIO MEETINGS.
I NEED TO TELL DAN I RAN INTO JOHN. WE AGREED TO THAT AND IT'S THE RIGHT THING TO DO.
ONE OF THEIR MAIN RULES WAS TO IMMEDIATELY TELL THE OTHER IF THIS HAPPENED.
HEY, BABE. HOW WAS YOUR PRESENTATION?
LIFESTYLE BLEEDING INTO OUR REAL LIVES WAS DAN'S BIGGEST CONCERN, BUT THINGS ARE GOING SO WELL...I DON'T WANT TO CREATE AN UNNECESSARY PROBLEM.
MAYBE I CAN ASK CLINT TO NOT MENTION IT?

SWINGING WAS MY IDEA AND IT TOOK DAN A LONG TIME TO GET INTO IT.
OUR DEVELOPING FRIENDSHIP WITH CLINT AND MARY WHO'VE BEEN IN LIFESTYLE A LOT LONGER HAS HELPED A LOT.
PRETTY NORMAL LOOKING HOUSE FOR PERVS, I'M A LITTLE DISAPPOINTED.
WHAT?
I'M KIDDING.
WELL, WELL, MISTER "I'M SO SERIOUS ABOUT ALL THIS"...THAT MAKES ME HAPPY, AT LEAST.
YOU NEVER JOKE AROUND WHEN YOU'RE NERVOUS.
NO LONGER AFRAID I'LL LEAVE YOU FOR ONE OF THESE MEN?
NAH, I TRUST YOU, BABE. IT WAS A FEAR, FOR SURE. I'M NOT SAYING IT WAS RATIONAL, BUT WHAT WE'RE DOING ISN'T NORMAL.
NORMAL FOR WHO? EVERYONE DECIDES WHAT WORKS FOR THEM.
DING DONG

DAN LIKES CLINT AND LOOKS UP TO HIM.
IT'S WHY I WAS SO SCARED WHEN I RAN INTO HIM AT THE STUDIO LAST MONTH.
WHY HELLO THERE, SEXY PEOPLE. COME ON IN!
DAN'S BIGGEST FEAR WAS LIFESTYLE SPILLING INTO OUR *"REAL"* LIFE.
WE BROUGHT SOME BUBBLY.
WE HAVE A GUEST ROOM IF IT GETS LATE AND YOU WANT TO SPEND THE NIGHT.
WE'D GIVE YOU PRIVACY AND YOU'D HAVE YOUR OWN BATH-ROOM.
APPRECIATE THE OFFER, BUT MY MOM IS WATCHING OUR KIDS AND EXPECTS US BY MIDNIGHT.

THE DAY AFTER I SAW HIM, I TEXTED CLINT ASKING HIM NOT TO MENTION IT. HE SAID HE WOULDN'T, BUT DISLIKED THE IDEA OF BEING DISHONEST.
DIRTY VEGAS IS COMING UP. WE GO EVERY YEAR AND WOULD LOVE IT IF YOU TWO CAME WITH US THIS TIME. IT'S A MASSIVE HOTEL TAKEOVER OF A CASINO AND SWINGERS FROM ALL OVER THE WORLD COME TO PARTY.
THAT SOUNDS AMAZING.
YEAH, YOU GET A BUNCH OF LIKEMINDED PEOPLE LIKE US TOGETHER AND IT CAN BE FUN...WILD SOMETIMES, BUT FUN.
WILD FUN SOUNDS LIKE A GOOD THING, WHAT DO YOU THINK, DAN?

I LIKE FUN.
THAT WAS FAST.

I'M AFRAID I'VE BEEN GONE ON BUSINESS A LOT LATELY; SHE MIGHT BE A LITTLE KEYED UP. LET'S GO TO THE OTHER ROOM.
UH, DAN? ARE YOU OKAY WITH THAT?

YEAH, SURE.

I HAVE A MINOR CONFESSION; BOTH MARY AND I ARE ON WHAT WE CALL OUR FUN COCKTAIL.
WHAT'S THAT?
MOLLY, POT, CAFFEINE, AND SOME RED WINE.
I'VE NEVER TRIED MOLLY. IS MIXING THAT STUFF SAFE?
WE'VE DONE IT FOR YEARS AND MICRODOSE. THE COMBINATION ALLOWS FOR CROSSFADING WHICH INTENSIFIES PLEASURE.

WATCHING MARY SO AGGRESSIVELY JUMP ON DAN MADE ME A LITTLE JEALOUS...
...AND IN A WAY I'M GLAD AS IT GIVES ME A MORE EMPATHIC UNDERSTANDING OF DAN'S STRUGGLES.
EVERYONE OKAY? ANYTHING WE SHOULD TALK ABOUT?
I'M GOOD.
I'M OKAY, BUT WE SHOULD GO. MY MOTHER HAS TEXTED ME TEN TIMES TO SEE WHEN WE'RE ON THE WAY.
WELL YOU TWO, I'M GLAD WE'VE GOTTEN TO KNOW YOU BETTER. WE SHOULD HANG OUT AGAIN SOON.
SPEAKING OF HANGING OUT, CATHY, I'LL BE ON THE LOT AGAIN THIS WEEK IF YOU WANT TO GRAB LUNCH.
UH... I'LL CHECK MY SCHEDULE AND LET YOU KNOW.
WAIT, WHAT?
WE SHOULD GO.
THANKS FOR COMING OVER, WE'LL SEE YOU SOON.

HE WAS AT ONE OF MY GROUP PRESENTATIONS ON THE LOT AND SAID HELLO AFTER. WE DID *NOT* HANG OUT.
I'M SORRY I DIDN'T TELL YOU EARLIER, BUT IT WAS NOTHING.
IF IT WERE NOTHING, YOU WOULD HAVE TOLD ME.
I WAS GOING TO, BUT I KNEW YOU'D OVERREACT, AND THINGS HAVE BEEN GOING SO WELL --
MAKES SENSE... IF IT WERE EASY, MORE PEOPLE WOULD DO IT.
-- OVERREACT? TO YOU SO CAVALIERLY BREECHING ONE OF OUR ESTABLISHED BOUNDARIES?
OH MY GOD, *STOP* WITH THE LITERARY HYPERBOLE. I DID NOT CAVALIERLY BREECH ANYTHING.
THIS ISN'T SHAKESPEARE, AND SOME OF YOUR BOUNDARIES ARE KIND OF RIDICULOUS.

WE MADE THOSE TOGETHER.
I AGREED TO THEM BECAUSE YOU WERE BEING SO PARANOID ABOUT EVERY-THING.
I MEAN, YOU PRETEND TO BE ME ONLINE TO TRY AND ENTRAP THESE GUYS INTO SAYING SOMETHING YOU DEEM INAPPROPRIATE SO YOU CAN VETO THEM. WHO *DOES* THAT?
I DIDN'T EVEN WANT TO DO THIS INITIALLY...BUT I TRIED IT BECAUSE I LOVE YOU AND I THOUGHT I COULD TRUST YOU.
YOU REALLY ARE BLOWING THIS INSANELY OUT OF PROPORTION.
THE EMOTIONAL HURDLES CAN BE DIFFICULT.
WHATEVER.

YOU DIDN'T EVEN APOLOGIZE.
YES, I DID. IT WAS ONE OF THE FIRST THINGS I SAID, YOU WERE CLEARLY TOO ANGRY TO HEAR IT.
WHY IS IT YOU'RE FINE PUSHING BOUNDARIES WHEN IT SUITS YOU, BUT WHEN I WANT TO IT'S LIKE PULLING TEETH?
WHAT IS THAT EVEN SUPPOSED TO MEAN? I NEVER ASKED FOR ANY OF THIS. I DID IT FOR YOU.
YOU DIDN'T SEEM TO MIND WHEN MARY WAS ALL OVER YOU.
WHO'S MARY?

ASK YOUR DAD.
YOU MAKE BLAKE AND I HUG IT OUT WHEN WE FIGHT, MAYBE YOU TWO SHOULD DO THE SAME.

YOU'D THINK SHE'D BE ON TIME FOR COUPLE'S THERAPY...JUST ONCE.
TWO MONTHS LATER
6:25
FRIDAY
SHE CHOSE FRIDAYS AT 6 SINCE HER ENTIRE INDUSTRY GOES TO HAPPY HOUR AND SHE FIGURED IT WOULD BE EASY TO SLIP OUT.
HER JOB IS MORE INTENSE THAN MINE, SO I TRY AND ACCOMMODATE...BUT IT'S FRUSTRATING FOR HER TO PICK THE APPOINTMENT AND STILL BE LATE.
SHE STILL HASN'T EVEN RESPONDED TO MY TEXT FROM TWO HOURS AGO REMINDING HER.
DAN, I'M SORRY, BUT IT'S BEEN A HALF HOUR. I'M AFRAID THIS SESSION IS CANCELLED, AND YOU'LL STILL BE BILLED FOR IT.
NO WORRIES, WE KNEW THAT WHEN WE SIGNED UP. SEE YOU NEXT WEEK HOPEFULLY.

THAT CATHY RAN INTO CLINT AT A MEETING DOESN'T BOTHER ME ALL THAT MUCH.
THAT SHE CONCEALED IT AND ENLISTED HIM TO HELP COVER IT UP BOTHERS ME AND MAKES ME WONDER IF THERE'S MORE TO IT.
IF HE HADN'T SCREWED UP AND REVEALED IT, WOULD I EVEN KNOW? DOES IT MATTER?
I'M A LIFELONG CHRONIC OVERTHINKER...I CAN'T HELP RUNNING SCENARIOS THROUGH MY MIND, REGARDLESS OF PLAUSIBILITY.
I'M SO SORRY, HONEY. THIS MEETING RAN LATE, AND THE CEO WAS THERE AND KEPT ASKING SPECIFIC QUESTIONS ABOUT MY THOUGHTS ON THE LONG-TERM VIABILITY OF THE COMPANY.
PLEASE LET ME MAKE IT UP TO YOU, DAN. I'LL HAVE MY MOM WATCH THE KIDS TONIGHT AND WE CAN GO OUT AND HAVE FUN TOGETHER. JUST THE TWO OF US.
I DON'T CARE IF WE EVER SWING AGAIN. I LOVE YOU.

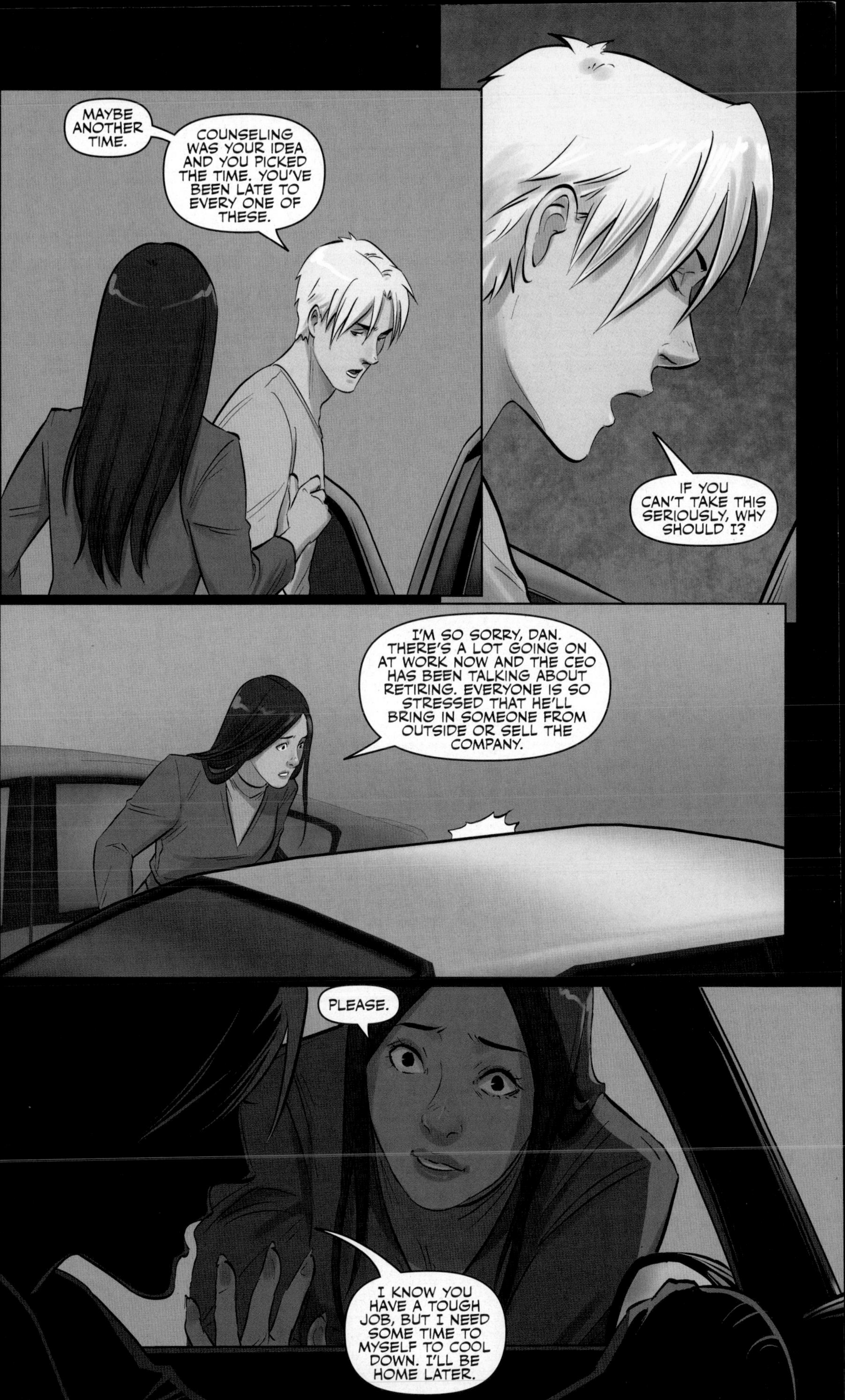
MAYBE ANOTHER TIME.
COUNSELING WAS YOUR IDEA AND YOU PICKED THE TIME. YOU'VE BEEN LATE TO EVERY ONE OF THESE.
IF YOU CAN'T TAKE THIS SERIOUSLY, WHY SHOULD I?
I'M SO SORRY, DAN. THERE'S A LOT GOING ON AT WORK NOW AND THE CEO HAS BEEN TALKING ABOUT RETIRING. EVERYONE IS SO STRESSED THAT HE'LL BRING IN SOMEONE FROM OUTSIDE OR SELL THE COMPANY.
PLEASE.
I KNOW YOU HAVE A TOUGH JOB, BUT I NEED SOME TIME TO MYSELF TO COOL DOWN. I'LL BE HOME LATER.

HE'S RIGHT TO BE UPSET.
IN MY ATTEMPT TO PREVENT A PROBLEM I VIOLATED A TRUST AND CREATED A MUCH WORSE PROBLEM.
FOR ME THERE ARE THREE THINGS IN THE WORLD THAT REALLY MATTER: FAMILY, CAREER, AND HEALTH. I NEED TWO OF THOSE TO BE WORKING WELL AT ANY GIVEN TIME.
AND I'M NOT SURE WHAT I CAN DO ABOUT MY WORK SITUATION.
IF THE COMPANY GETS ACQUIRED OR SOMEONE NEW COMES IN, I COULD BE OUT OF A JOB.
THAT ON TOP OF THIS MARITAL STRESS IS KILLING ME.

AM I OVERREACTING TO ALL THIS? PROBABLY.
I DON'T WANT TO GET DIVORCED AND I LOVE HER, BUT THIS SWINGING STUFF IS HARD TO HANDLE EMOTIONALLY AT TIMES.
I GET JEALOUS AT SUCH LITTLE THINGS, BUT IT'S GETTING EASIER... ESPECIALLY IF I REALLY LIKE THE COUPLE.
MAYBE SWINGING WAS A MISTAKE, BUT WHAT'S THE ALTERNATIVE? WILL CATHY ACCEPT MY ENDING IT? OR WILL SHE JUST SECRETLY BE MAD AT ME ABOUT IT AND LET IT FESTER UNTIL SHE CHEATS ON ME FOR REAL.
HEY, HANDSOME.
TRUST IS A HARD THING. EVEN THE SMALLEST OF INFRACTIONS CAN CAUSE YOU TO QUESTION EVERYTHING.
I'M DAN, IT'S NICE TO MEET YOU...?
SARA.

CAN I BUY YOU A DRINK, SARA?
YES, PLEASE, I'M DRINKING THE BLOND ALE, WHATEVER IT'S CALLED.

TWO HOURS LATER
I THINK THAT'S IT FOR ME, I NEED TO GET HOME.
IT'S NOT EVEN MIDNIGHT YET.
I love you. Please don't be mad at me. I'm so sorry I was late. I'll talk to the bosses and tell them I can't stay past 5 on fridays.
DAN, I'M GOING TO BE BLUNT. I JUST GOT OUT OF A LONG-TERM CAUSTIC RELATIONSHIP AND I AM LOOKING FOR A FUCK BUDDY, NOTHING SERIOUS.
YOU GAME TO HOOK UP, NO STRINGS ATTACHED?

11:45
DAN
I love you. Please don't be mad at me. I'm so sorry I was late. I'll talk to the bosses and tell them I can't stay past 5 on fridays.
HE'S NEVER JUST NOT RESPONDED TO ME LIKE THIS.
I NEVER REALIZED HOW IMPORTANT IT WAS FOR ME TO HAVE DAN'S COMPLETE SUPPORT.
I'VE NEVER NOT HAD IT...UNTIL NOW... AND IT SUCKS.
HI.

OH, DAN, I LOVE YOU. I'M SO SORRY.

WOW.

THAT WAS UNEXPECTED.
LOTS MORE WHERE THAT CAME FROM, BUT WE NEED TO REINSTITUTE OUR DATE NIGHTS.
WE NEED MORE QUALITY TIME FOR JUST US.
A WOMAN TRIED TO TAKE ME HOME TONIGHT, BUT NOTHING HAPPENED.
DID YOU GET HER NUMBER?
BEEN A WHILE SINCE WE HAD A GOOD OLD-FASHIONED THREESOME.

ORLANDO, FLORIDA.
THE LAST FEW MONTHS HAVE FLOWN BY. DAN AND I HAVE RECONNECTED AND ARE ON A GOOD PATH TOGETHER ONCE AGAIN.
WE HAVE NOT TRIED TO SWING AGAIN AND I'M OKAY WITH THAT.
I DO ENJOY THAT LIFESTYLE, BUT IT'S IMPORTANT TO REMEMBER WHAT REALLY MATTERS AND FOCUS MY TIME AND ENERGY THERE.
FAMILY IS EVERYTHING TO ME.
CAN WE TRY THAT RING TOSS GAME AGAIN, MOM? I WANT TO WIN THAT GIANT TURTLE.
MAYBE LATER.
NO ON WINS TH GAME, RIGGE
CATHY WON LAST YEAR AT THE LA COUNTY FAIR.
LUCK ISN'T WINNING.
THIS IS A HAPPY PLACE, WHY SO GLUM? LET'S GO ON THE WATER RIDE!

YEEAAHH!
YOU SUCK, BLAKE. LOOK AT MY SCORE.
WHATEVER, DUMB BUTT, MY CANNON ISN'T WORKING RIGHT.

THOSE FIREWORKS WERE SO COOL. I WISH WE COULD COME HERE EVERY DAY.
OKAY KIDDOS, YOU'RE CRASHING WITH GRANDMA TONIGHT, SO YOUR DAD AND I CAN HAVE SOME TIME TOGETHER.
YOU'D RATHER HAVE SEX THAN HANG OUT WITH YOUR CHILDREN?
I'M IGNORING THAT, ASHLEY.
<DON'T GET PREGNANT. WE DON'T NEED A THIRD ONE OF THESE.>*
*TRANSLATED FROM MANDARIN.
WHAT'D SHE SAY?
JUST TO HAVE A GOOD TIME.
YOU WANT TO GO OUT OR SHOULD WE GET A BOTTLE OF WINE AND STAY IN?
WELL... I KNOW IT'S BEEN A WHILE, AND YOU CAN SAY NO AND I WON'T BE UPSET...
...BUT THERE'S A LIFESTYLE CLUB HERE IF YOU WANT TO GO CHECK IT OUT.

I'M A LITTLE LEERY TO JUMP BACK INTO THIS SWINGING STUFF, BUT THINGS ARE GOOD WITH CATH AGAIN...AND WE ARE ON VACATION...
THAT COUPLE THERE IS EYEBALLING US.
...SO WHAT THE HELL!
I'VE NEVER BEEN WITH A BLACK GIRL BEFORE.
BUCKET LIST?
ACTUALLY, I NEVER REALLY THOUGHT ABOUT SWINGING IN OTHER CITIES.
THE IDEA HOLDS GREATER APPEAL TO ME. IT'S NOT LIKE WE'D EVER RUN INTO THESE PEOPLE IN A GROCERY STORE.
SOUNDS GOOD TO ME.
HEY THERE, I'M CHRIS AND THIS IS MY WIFE DONICA.
ARE YOU INTO GIRLS?

A LITTLE BIT, I'VE NOT HAD MUCH EXPERIENCE.
ORAL FROM A WOMAN WHO'S REALLY INTO IT IS OUT OF THIS WORLD.
ARE YOU REALLY INTO IT?
YES.
I'D NEED DAN'S APPROVAL IF WE INVOLVE YOUR HUSBAND...
...BUT HE'S BUSY... AND HE DOESN'T CARE IF I'M WITH A WOMAN.
SHOW ME.
I'M GOING TO ROCK YOUR WORLD.

CAN WE PLAY, TOO?

THE KEY TO SWINGING IS TO NOT GIVE A SHIT ABOUT THE PERSON YOU BROUGHT.
THAT WOULD BE DIFFICULT FOR ME SINCE CATHY IS MY WIFE.
I HAVE A WIFE, TOO, BUT I BRING THIS SUGAR BABY WITH ME ON VACATIONS. *
*THIS GUY IS THE DOUCHEBAG FROM SUGAR V1.
WHAT'S A SUGAR BABY?
IT'S THE BEST OF EVERYTHING. A HOT, YOUNGER WOMAN WHO ACCOMPANIES YOU, HAS SEX WITH YOU AND DOES WHAT SHE'S TOLD.
ALL THAT FOR A FEW GRAND A MONTH.
YOU PAY HER FOR SEX?
IT'S LIKE CHARLIE SHEEN SAYS, YOU PAY THEM TO LEAVE AND NOT BE A NUISANCE. BELIEVE ME, IT'S WORTH EVERY PENNY.

HONEY, WE NEED TO GO, DID YOU GET A CHANCE TO MEET...I'M SORRY, WHAT DID YOU SAY YOUR NAME WAS?
RICHARD, BUT YOU CAN CALL ME DICK.
I'M IN LOS ANGELES ALSO. PASADENA AREA. CANDY AND I'D BE DOWN FOR A PLAY DATE. HIT US UP.
DICK, OH MY GOD, THAT'S SO APPROPRIATE. THAT GUY DEFINES DICKHEAD. AND HIS SUGAR BABY, CANDY? THAT'S LIKE STRAIGHT OUT OF A BAD PORNO.
SHE WAS HOT AND BARELY 21. I'D DO A PLAY DATE IF YOU WANTED TO HIT THAT.
THAT'S THE DEFINITION OF "TAKING ONE FOR THE TEAM" AND NO THANKS. I'D LIKE TO NEVER HAVE AN IMAGE IN MY MIND OF THAT GUY ON TOP OF YOU.
TAKE ME TO BED AND FINISH ME OFF THEN, STUD?

HEY SPORT, IT'S BEEN A LONG TIME, HOW'S IT HANGING?
A BIT TO THE LEFT, HEH, YOU'RE ONE OF THE FEW GUYS THAT KNOWS THAT.
ALL PART OF OUR SECRET SOCIETY.
I LIKE THAT. MAKES IT SOUND LIKE WE'RE IN A SPECIAL CLUB OR SOMETHING.
I'M SORRY ABOUT WHAT HAPPENED. MARY AND I WERE A LITTLE ALTERED FOR THAT LAST SESSION AND I SHOULD NEVER HAVE AGREED TO KEEP THAT QUIET IN THE FIRST PLACE.
THAT'S ON ME AND I WANT YOU TO KNOW THAT MY INTENT WAS PURELY SOCIAL. I'D NEVER HIT ON CATHY OR TRY TO GET ANYTHING GOING THAT YOU WEREN'T OKAY WITH.
I APPRECIATE ALL THAT MORE THAN YOU COULD POSSIBLY REALIZE.

GOOD TO SEE YOU. I WAS WORRIED AFTER CLINT TOLD ME WHAT HAPPENED. CLINT WAS BESIDE HIMSELF, HE FELT STUPID FOR LETTING THAT HAPPEN.
HE REALLY LIKES YOU GUYS AND REAL FRIENDS IN LIFESTYLE ARE HARD TO COME BY.
WE NEEDED TO WORK A COUPLE THINGS OUT. WE REALLY LIKE YOU GUYS, TOO.
THAT MAKES ME HAPPY.
CARE TO WAGER THAT YOU CAN'T HIT FURTHER THAN I JUST DID?
I'M NOT MUCH OF A GAMBLER.
BUT IF I WIN, YOU HAVE TO COME TO A SCHOOLGIRL PARTY WE'RE GOING TO THIS WEEKEND.
SOUNDS NAUGHTY, I'M IN.
LOOKS LIKE YOU WIN THIS ONE.
WIDEN YOUR STANCE AND LIFT YOUR LEFT HEEL DURING THE BACKSWING AND YOU'LL HIT FARTHER.

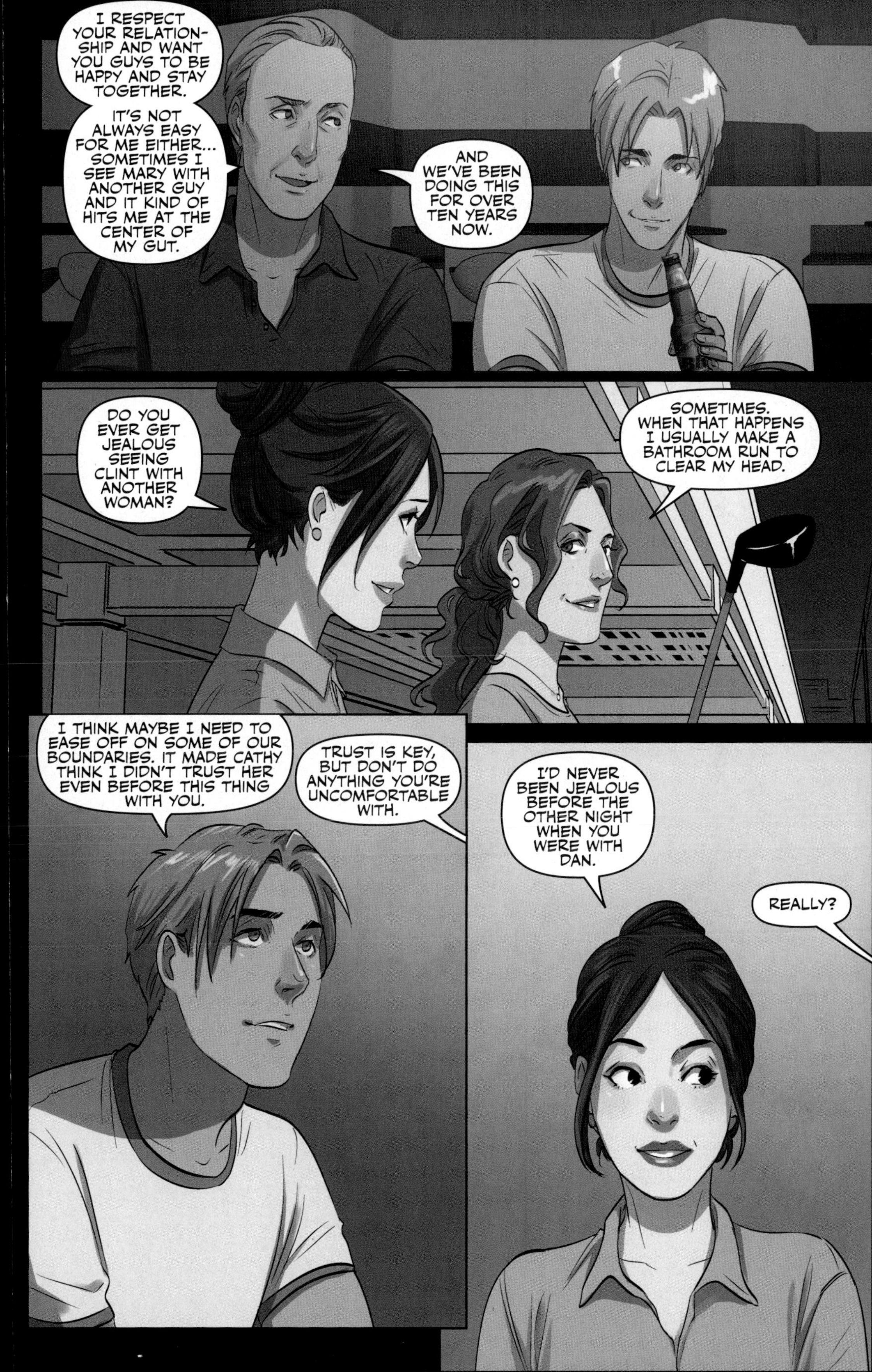
I RESPECT YOUR RELATIONSHIP AND WANT YOU GUYS TO BE HAPPY AND STAY TOGETHER.
IT'S NOT ALWAYS EASY FOR ME EITHER... SOMETIMES I SEE MARY WITH ANOTHER GUY AND IT KIND OF HITS ME AT THE CENTER OF MY GUT.
AND WE'VE BEEN DOING THIS FOR OVER TEN YEARS NOW.
DO YOU EVER GET JEALOUS SEEING CLINT WITH ANOTHER WOMAN?
SOMETIMES. WHEN THAT HAPPENS I USUALLY MAKE A BATHROOM RUN TO CLEAR MY HEAD.
I THINK MAYBE I NEED TO EASE OFF ON SOME OF OUR BOUNDARIES. IT MADE CATHY THINK I DIDN'T TRUST HER EVEN BEFORE THIS THING WITH YOU.
TRUST IS KEY, BUT DON'T DO ANYTHING YOU'RE UNCOMFORTABLE WITH.
I'D NEVER BEEN JEALOUS BEFORE THE OTHER NIGHT WHEN YOU WERE WITH DAN.
REALLY?

ONE THING CERTAIN ABOUT AT I'D NEVER O GO BACK TO OGAMY. LIFE'S T AND NO ONE SON CAN BE RYTHING TO EONE ELSE.
I CAN BE HONEST WITH MY WIFE ABOUT MY FANTASIES AND DESIRES AND WE EXPLORE OUR SEXUALITY TOGETHER. AND FOR THE FOUR OF US TO BE PLAY BUDDIES LONG TERM, YOU AND I'LL NEED TO BE HONEST WITH EACH OTHER AS WELL.
BELIEVE ME, IT GETS WAY EASIER THE LONGER YOU'RE IN IT. YOU ALSO DEVELOP A SIXTH SENSE ABOUT THE PEOPLE THAT WILL BE DIFFICULT. WE'VE HAD MORE DRAMA WITH OTHER WOMEN THAN MEN.
A LOT OF PEOPLE TRY SWINGING BECAUSE THEIR RELATIONSHIP IS IN TROUBLE. SWINGING WILL NEVER WORK FOR THEM AND IT ALMOST ALWAYS ENDS TRAGICALLY.
TAKE IT SLOW AND SEE WHAT WORKS FOR YOU. I KNOW COUPLES THAT DO THIS ONCE A YEAR JUST TO SCRATCH THE ITCH AND I KNOW OTHERS THAT IT'S A FULL-TIME HOBBY FOR AND ARE HOOKING UP MULTIPLE TIMES A WEEK.
YEAH, I WAS JEALOUS OF YOU FOR A MINUTE THERE.
YA KNOW, IN HINDSIGHT WE SHOULD HAVE LAID OFF THE MOLLY. I LOVE IT BECAUSE IT MAKES SEX SO AMAZING, BUT IT DOES MAKE ME MORE AGGRESSIVE AND AFFECTIONATE. SORRY IF THAT CAUSED AN ISSUE.
NEXT TIME YOU SHOULD DO IT WITH US.
DAN WOULD NEVER DO DRUGS LIKE THAT, SO I'LL HAVE TO PASS.

IT'S BEEN AWHILE SINCE I'VE CAUSED A WIPE.
ALLY AND VLAD ARE SO INTENSE ABOUT IT, BUT THEY DO THE RESEARCH AND REALLY TAKE IT SERIOUSLY AND I JUST DO WHAT THEY SAY WHICH MAKES IT EASY FOR ME.
RAIDING IN THIS GAME WITH THESE GUYS IS THE ONE THING I GET ALL TO MYSELF THAT HAS NOTHING TO DO WITH WORK, LIFESTYLE, FAMILY...EVERYTHING. I NEED IT.
IT'S WEIRD. I'VE NEVER MET THESE PEOPLE, BUT WE TALK AND INTERACT LIKE OLD FRIENDS.
THE DOOR SAYS, "OPEN THE GATEWAY AND A BLESSING OF LIGHT WILL FALL UPON YOU."
THAT SHOULD OPEN THE DOOR.
LET'S DO THIS, GUYS! SERVER FIRST IF WE GET THIS OPEN.

BE READY FOR ANYTHING.
LET'S REBUFF BEFORE WE GO IN.
WE SHOULD HAVE DONE THAT BEFORE YOU OPENED THE DOOR.
ARE WE SURE THAT MIST ISN'T HARMFUL?
IF IT IS, WE CAN RES* AT THE PORTAL IN THE LAST ROOM.
*RESURRECT
WE DID IT, DUDE, SERVER FIRST! HIGH FIVE!
UH, I DON'T KNOW HOW TO MAKE MY CHARACTER DO THAT.
IT'S ON YOUR SOCIAL PAGE UNDER EMOTES. YOU CAN HOTKEY IT.

INCOMING! THEY'RE ALL ELITE MOBS.
TODAY IS A GOOD DAY TO DIE!

WELP! WE DID GREAT, BUT WE LOST FOCUS AT THE END. SO CLOSE!
THAT WAS FUN, YOU GUYS. I CAN'T WAIT TO GO BRAG IN THE FORUMS.
FOCUS?! DAN WAS TAKING FIFTY THOUSAND DAMAGE PER SECOND, I COULDN'T POSSIBLY HEAL THROUGH THAT! THOSE MOBS WERE INSANE!
WE'LL HAVE TO TRY SOME DIFFERENT THINGS, MAYBE THEY CAN BE DEBUFFED.

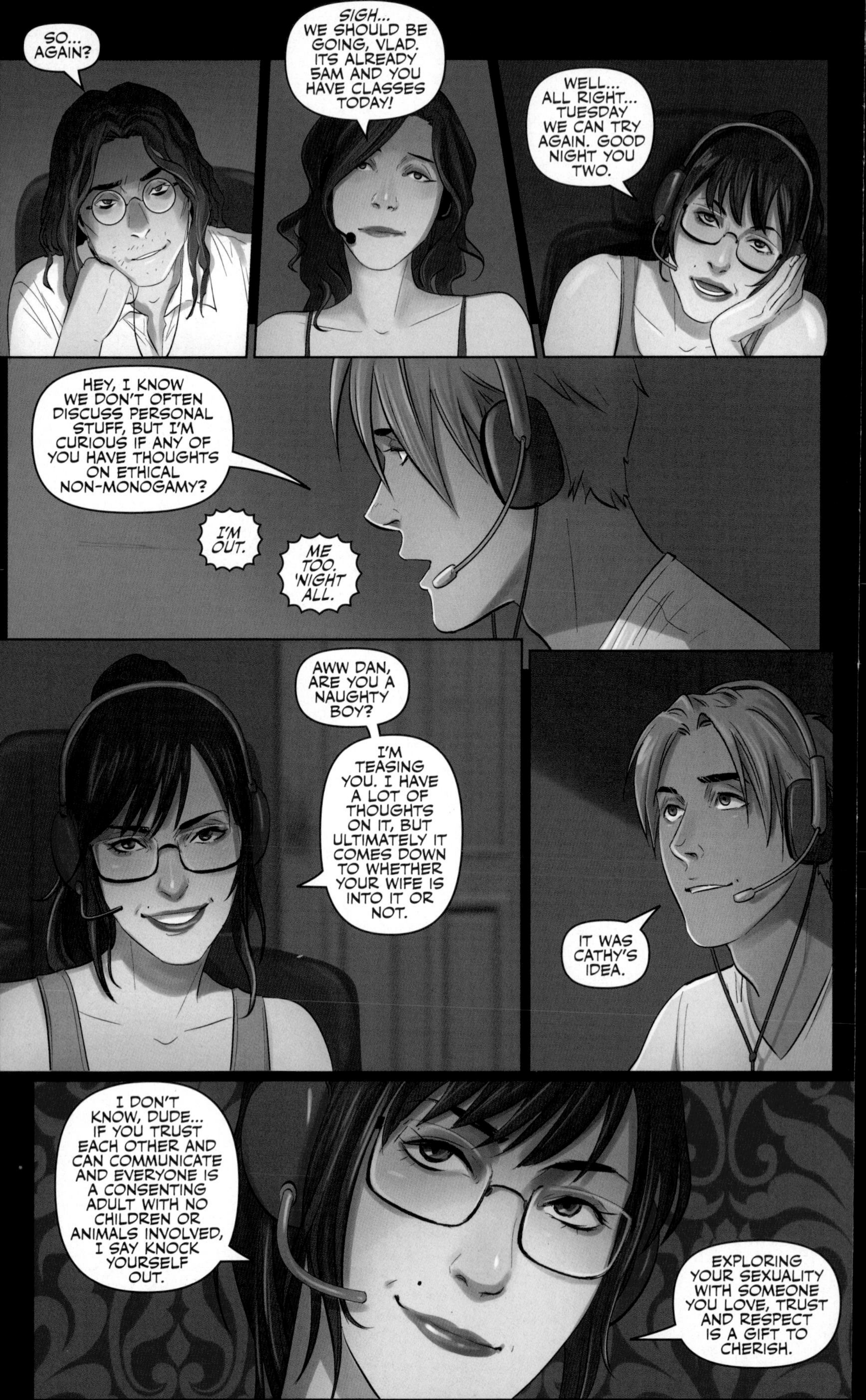
SO... AGAIN?
SIGH... WE SHOULD BE GOING, VLAD. ITS ALREADY 5AM AND YOU HAVE CLASSES TODAY!
WELL... ALL RIGHT... TUESDAY WE CAN TRY AGAIN. GOOD NIGHT YOU TWO.
HEY, I KNOW WE DON'T OFTEN DISCUSS PERSONAL STUFF, BUT I'M CURIOUS IF ANY OF YOU HAVE THOUGHTS ON ETHICAL NON-MONOGAMY?
I'M OUT.
ME TOO. 'NIGHT ALL.
AWW DAN, ARE YOU A NAUGHTY BOY?
I'M TEASING YOU. I HAVE A LOT OF THOUGHTS ON IT, BUT ULTIMATELY IT COMES DOWN TO WHETHER YOUR WIFE IS INTO IT OR NOT.
IT WAS CATHY'S IDEA.
I DON'T KNOW, DUDE... IF YOU TRUST EACH OTHER AND CAN COMMUNICATE AND EVERYONE IS A CONSENTING ADULT WITH NO CHILDREN OR ANIMALS INVOLVED, I SAY KNOCK YOURSELF OUT.
EXPLORING YOUR SEXUALITY WITH SOMEONE YOU LOVE, TRUST AND RESPECT IS A GIFT TO CHERISH.

SANTA MONICA, CALIFORNIA.
NICE HOUSE.
IF WE DIDN'T HAVE THOSE TWO HOOVERS AT HOME TO FEED AND MY MOM TO SUPPORT WE COULD PROBABLY UPGRADE.
NAH, I'M HAPPY WITH OUR LIFE.
YEAH? YOU LIKE YOUR LITTLE SCHOOL-GIRL?
INDEED, I DO.
THEY'VE GOT SOME RICH FRIENDS. THAT ODDLY MAKES ME A BIT JEALOUS.
THAT'S FUNNY I WAS THINKING THE SAME THING.
YOU'RE POPPING A VIAGRA THIS EARLY?
BETTER SAFE THAN SORRY.
THAT'S KINDA HOT.

HEY, YOU TWO!
HEY, HEY! LOOK WHO IT IS. THANKS FOR COMING.
THEY HAVEN'T CUM YET, DEAR, THE NIGHT IS YOUNG.
AND *I'M* THE JOKESTER?
IS IT WEIRD THAT DAN AND I ARE A LITTLE JEALOUS OF YOUR FANCY FRIENDS?
NOT AT ALL, WE'RE AWESOME. YOU CAN MAKE SOME NEW FRIENDS TONIGHT.
I CAN VOUCH FOR EVERYONE HERE.

HOW LONG HAVE YOU BEEN IN LIFESTYLE?
ABOUT A YEAR, BUT WE TOOK A BREAK IN THE MIDDLE.

TWO HOURS LATER.
CLINT TOLD ME YOU'RE A WRITER. YOU WRITE MOVIES OR TV?
NEITHER, I'M WORKING ON A NOVEL BUT I DON'T HAVE A PUBLISHER YET.
I'M AN AGENT OVER AT WMC AND WE'VE GOT LITERARY AGENTS THAT MIGHT BE ABLE TO HELP YOU OUT.
THAT WOULD BE GREAT. I'D APPRECIATE IT.
IS THE PARTY WINDING DOWN? IT SEEMS MOST PEOPLE HAVE LEFT ALREADY.
EVERYONE IS UPSTAIRS IN THE PUPPY PILE ROOM. WE'RE ABOUT TO HEAD UP NOW.
WHAT'S THAT?
THE ORGY ROOM.
REALLY?

WOW, I REALLY DON'T WANT TO LET CATHY DOWN. I KNOW SHE'S EXCITED BY THIS, BUT THE IDEA OF AN ORGY FILLS ME WITH SHEER TERROR.
I'M NOT READY FOR THIS, BUT MAYBE I SHOULD JUST DO IT FOR HER.
NO. HONEST COMMUNICATION IS KEY. I NEED TO VOICE MY FEAR.
SHALL WE DIVE IN?
I CAN CLEARLY SEE THAT THIS IS SOMETHING YOU WANT TO TRY.

I LOVE YOU AND WANT TO BE ABLE TO TRY THESE THINGS TOGETHER... BUT I'M JUST NOT READY FOR THIS YET, HONEY.
I'M SORRY.
THANK YOU FOR TELLING ME THE WAY YOU DID. I LOVE YOU TOO, BABE.

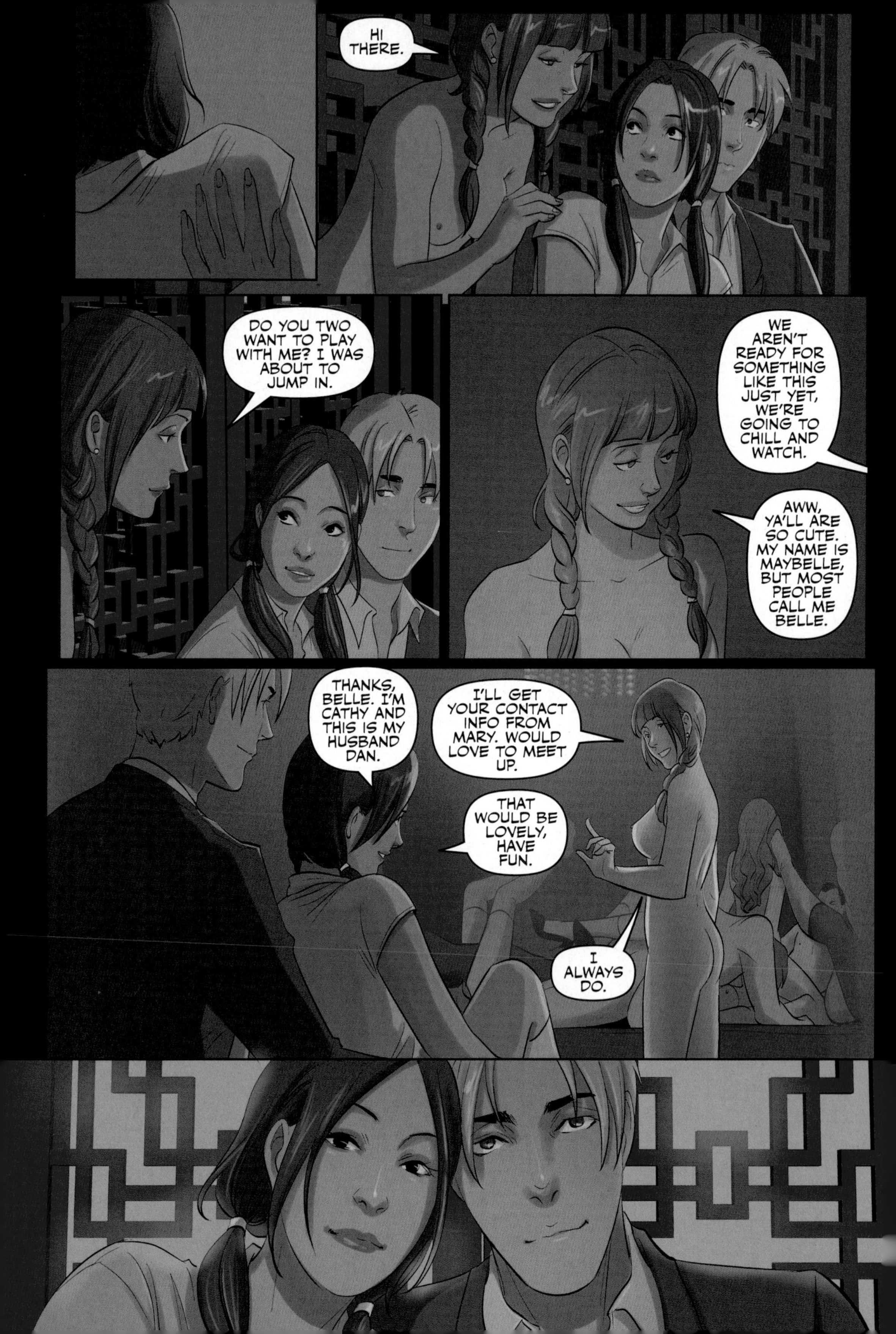
HI THERE.
DO YOU TWO WANT TO PLAY WITH ME? I WAS ABOUT TO JUMP IN.
WE AREN'T READY FOR SOMETHING LIKE THIS JUST YET, WE'RE GOING TO CHILL AND WATCH.
AWW, YA'LL ARE SO CUTE. MY NAME IS MAYBELLE, BUT MOST PEOPLE CALL ME BELLE.
THANKS, BELLE. I'M CATHY AND THIS IS MY HUSBAND DAN.
I'LL GET YOUR CONTACT INFO FROM MARY. WOULD LOVE TO MEET UP.
THAT WOULD BE LOVELY, HAVE FUN.
I ALWAYS DO.

SIX MONTHS OF WORK ALL DOWN TO THIS ONE MOMENT.
I DID IT!
WHAT'D YOU DO, DAD?
CATAN
I SUBMITTED MY BOOK TO SEVERAL PUBLISHERS.

ARE YOU GOING TO BE LIKE STEPHEN KING NOW?

HEH, I WISH, BUT PROBABLY NOT.
YOUR MOM AND I ARE HAVING DINNER WITH GRANDPA SO I'M DROPPING YOU OFF AT GRANDMAS. SHE'S MAKING YOU DINNER.

AW MAN, DO WE HAVE TO? IT'S GOING TO BE ASIAN FOOD ***AGAIN.***
YOU'RE SUCH A RACIST.
I'M HALF CHINESE, I CAN'T BE RACIST AGAINST ASIANS.
YES, YOU ***CAN,*** MORON.
IDIOT!
RACIST!
NOTHING LIKE A PAIR OF SCREAMING KIDS AND MY MOTHER-IN-LAW TO CELEBRATE MY CAREER MILESTONE.
FOR SUCH A SMALL AND FRAIL OLD WOMAN, SHE SCARES THE BEJEEZUS OUT OF ME.

THANKS SO MUCH FOR WATCHING THEM, WE CAN PICK THEM UP AFTER 11 OR IN THE MORNING.
MORNING IS FINE.
DAN, I'VE BEEN MEANING TO TALK TO YOU ABOUT CATHY.
I'M REALLY CONCERNED THAT SHE DOESN'T SPEND ENOUGH TIME WITH THE CHILDREN. THEY NEED THEIR MOTHER.
WILL YOU TELL HER TO QUIT HER JOB SO SHE CAN STAY HOME AND BE A MOTHER LIKE SHE'S SUPPOSED TO BE?
I DON'T THINK THAT WOULD GO OVER VERY WELL WITH CATHY. I DON'T TELL HER WHAT TO DO.
不能像妻管严一样，你应该当家作主。
UH... HAVE A NICE NIGHT AND THANKS.

HEY, CAROL, IS CATH IN HER OFFICE?
NOPE. SHE'S IN THE CONFERENCE ROOM.
CONGRATS, BY THE WAY, WE'RE ALL EXCITED ABOUT THE NEWS.
HEY EVERYONE, WHAT'S GOING ON?
HEY, BABE! COME HAVE A GLASS OF CHAMPAGNE WITH US.
DAN, YOU ARE THE LUCKIEST GUY IN THE WORLD TO BE MARRIED TO THIS WOMAN.
I'VE DECIDED TO RETIRE, AND I'VE NAMED CATHY AS MY SUCCESSOR.
I'LL BE LEAVING THE COMPANY I FOUNDED FORTY YEARS AGO IN HER CAPABLE HANDS.

I JUST FOUND OUT AN HOUR AGO, SORRY TO SPRING IT ON YOU LIKE THIS.
CONGRATULATIONS, HONEY, I'M SO PROUD OF YOU.
REALLY? YOU'RE NOT UPSET. IT'LL MEAN MORE HOURS, TRAVEL.
WE'LL FIGURE IT OUT.
GET A ROOM!

RE YOU ERVOUS ABOUT ING YOUR ? WHEN'S HE LAST ME YOU ALKED?
ABOUT A YEAR AGO. THINGS HAVE NOT BEEN GOOD WITH HIM SINCE HE BAILED ON MY MOM.
THAT WAS TWENTY YEARS AGO.
I KNOW.
DID HE SAY WHAT HE WANTED?
JUST THAT HE HAD BIG NEWS AND NOT TO BRING THE KIDS.
THAT SOUNDS OMINOUS.
I KNOW, RIGHT?
HEY, DAN, CATHY, YOU GUYS LOOK FANTASTIC! THIS IS MY GIRLFRIEND ELIZABETH.
CALL ME LIZ.
IT'S GOOD TO SEE YOU, OLD MAN.
NOT TOO OLD TO TRY AGAIN, WE'RE ENGAGED.
THAT'S WONDERFUL NEWS, I'M HAPPY FOR YOU BOTH.

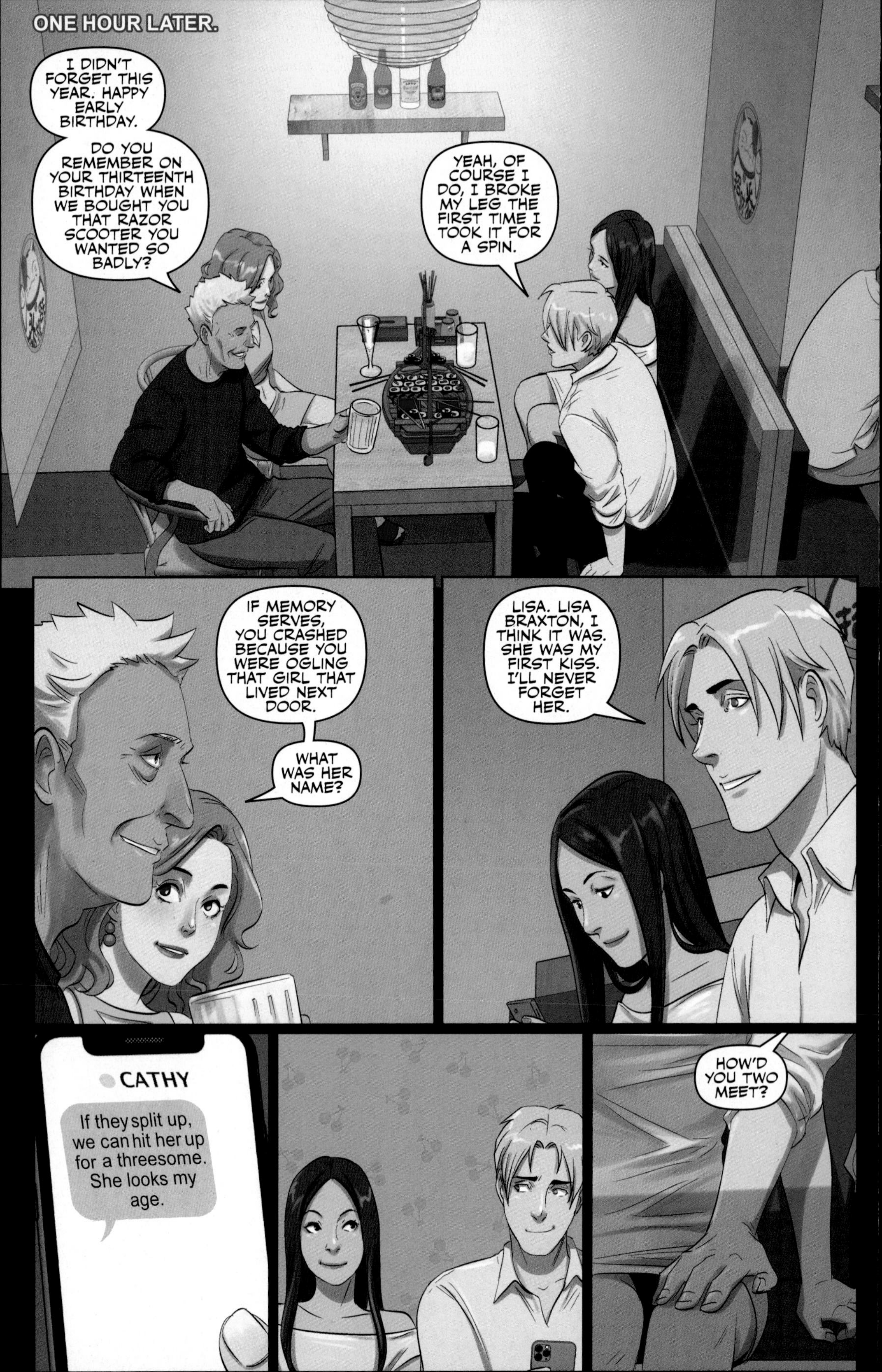
ONE HOUR LATER.
I DIDN'T FORGET THIS YEAR. HAPPY EARLY BIRTHDAY.
DO YOU REMEMBER ON YOUR THIRTEENTH BIRTHDAY WHEN WE BOUGHT YOU THAT RAZOR SCOOTER YOU WANTED SO BADLY?
YEAH, OF COURSE I DO, I BROKE MY LEG THE FIRST TIME I TOOK IT FOR A SPIN.
IF MEMORY SERVES, YOU CRASHED BECAUSE YOU WERE OGLING THAT GIRL THAT LIVED NEXT DOOR.
WHAT WAS HER NAME?
LISA. LISA BRAXTON, I THINK IT WAS. SHE WAS MY FIRST KISS. I'LL NEVER FORGET HER.
CATHY
If they split up, we can hit her up for a threesome. She looks my age.
HOW'D YOU TWO MEET?

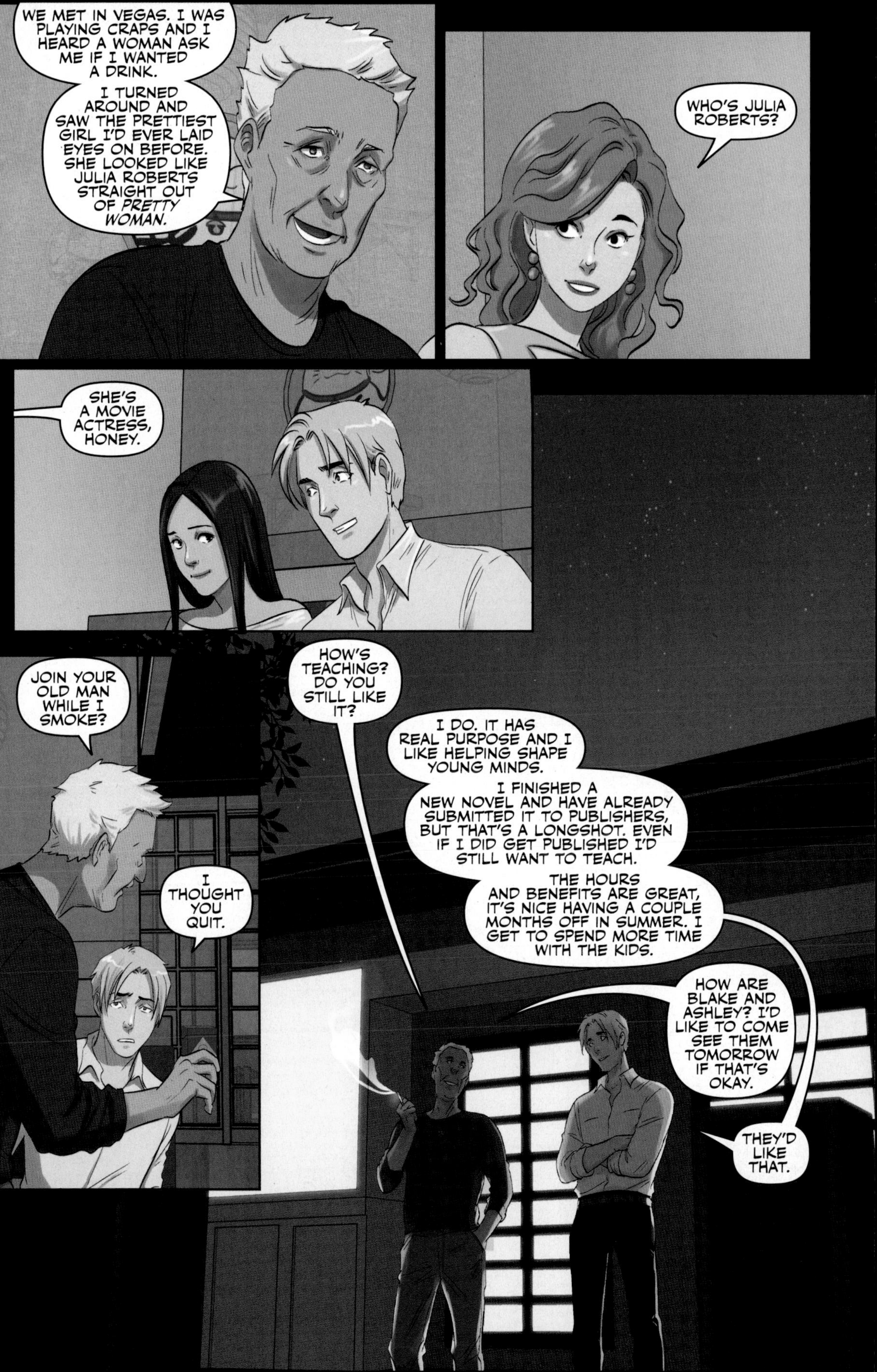
WE MET IN VEGAS. I WAS PLAYING CRAPS AND I HEARD A WOMAN ASK ME IF I WANTED A DRINK.
I TURNED AROUND AND SAW THE PRETTIEST GIRL I'D EVER LAID EYES ON BEFORE. SHE LOOKED LIKE JULIA ROBERTS STRAIGHT OUT OF *PRETTY WOMAN.*
WHO'S JULIA ROBERTS?
SHE'S A MOVIE ACTRESS, HONEY.
JOIN YOUR OLD MAN WHILE I SMOKE?
I THOUGHT YOU QUIT.
HOW'S TEACHING? DO YOU STILL LIKE IT?
I DO. IT HAS REAL PURPOSE AND I LIKE HELPING SHAPE YOUNG MINDS.
I FINISHED A NEW NOVEL AND HAVE ALREADY SUBMITTED IT TO PUBLISHERS, BUT THAT'S A LONGSHOT. EVEN IF I DID GET PUBLISHED I'D STILL WANT TO TEACH.
THE HOURS AND BENEFITS ARE GREAT, IT'S NICE HAVING A COUPLE MONTHS OFF IN SUMMER. I GET TO SPEND MORE TIME WITH THE KIDS.
HOW ARE BLAKE AND ASHLEY? I'D LIKE TO COME SEE THEM TOMORROW IF THAT'S OKAY.
THEY'D LIKE THAT.

SHARE YOUR SECRET WITH ME. YOU'VE BEEN MARRIED TO CATHY LONGER THAN I WAS TO ANY OF MY WIVES. HOW DO YOU MAKE IT WORK? I REALLY LIKE LIZ; I KNOW SHE'S YOUNG BUT WE GET ALONG SO WELL IT'S THE EASIEST RELATIONSHIP I'VE EVER HAD.
THERE'S NO MAGIC SECRET, WE'VE HAD OUR FAIR SHARE OF PROBLEMS. WE EVEN WENT THROUGH MARITAL COUNSELING RECENTLY.
ULTIMATELY, IT'S ABOUT LOVE, TRUST, COMMUNICATION, RESPECT...AND PUTTING IN THE TIME.
I LOVE CATHY WITH ALL MY HEART AND WANT HER AND THE KIDS TO BE HAPPY.
I'D DO ANYTHING FOR THEM.
CATHY AND I ALSO HAVE REGULAR DATE NIGHTS WITHOUT THE KIDS SO THAT OUR RELATIONSHIP DOESN'T GET LOST IN THE FAMILY DYNAMIC.
I'M PROUD OF YOU, DAN. YOU'VE GROWN INTO A FINE MAN.
AND ON THAT NOTE, I HAVE SOMETHING I WANT TO GIVE YOU. CAN YOU SWING BY MY HOTEL LATER? LIKE 9ISH? LIZ IS GOING TO SEE SOME FRIENDS, SO JUST COME IN.
IT'S GOOD TO SEE YOU, DAN. I HOPE WE CAN SPEND MORE TIME TOGETHER IN THE FUTURE.

MARY TEXTED AND ASKED IF YOU WANTED A THREESOME WITH HER TOMORROW NIGHT FOR YOUR BIRTHDAY.
NAH, THREESOMES ARE LIKE A REGULAR SATURDAY NIGHT NOW. I'D RATHER SPEND TIME WITH YOU AND THE KIDS.
I'LL GIVE YOU A NICE BIRTHDAY TREAT.
MAYBE I'LL BLOW YOU WHILE YOU'RE GAMING.
MY MOM CALLED, AND BLAKE NEEDS HIS ALLERGY MEDICATION, CAN YOU RUN THAT OVER REALLY QUICK BEFORE YOU GO SEE YOUR DAD?
CAN'T YOU DO IT? YOUR MOM SCARES ME.
PLEASE, I HAVE TO RUN BACK TO WORK BEFORE I CAN COME HOME SO THAT I WON'T HAVE TO WORK AT ALL THIS WEEKEND.
SURE.

I dropped off the meds. I'm at the hotel now.
404
I don't think I'll be long.
Happy Birthday DAN
SINCE THREESOMES ARE, SO PASSÉ FOR YOU NOW.

MY BIRTHDAY ISN'T UNTIL TOMORROW.
WE'RE NOT GOING TO LET YOU CUM UNTIL AFTER MIDNIGHT.
HAPPY BIRTHDAY.
MAKE A WISH, IT JUST MIGHT COME TRUE.
Happy Birthday

THE QUIET MOMENTS LIKE THIS MAKE LIFE WORTH LIVING.
WATCHING DAN WITH THE KIDS MAKES ME REALIZE HOW LUCKY I AM TO HAVE FOUND A GOOD MAN LIKE HIM.
I DON'T WANT ANYTHING TO COME BETWEEN HE AND I EVER AGAIN.
GOOD JOB, SHIT FOR BRAINS.
ASHLEY! WATCH THE LANGUAGE OR WE'LL GO HOME NOW.
SORRY, MOM. DAD SAYS "SHIT" ALL THE TIME.

I DO, YA KNOW. I'LL TRY TO STOP.
I'M SURE THEY HEAR MUCH WORSE EVERY DAY AT SCHOOL.
IS THIS WINE?
WE AREN'T DRIVING, SO WHAT THE HELL?
LOOK AT YOU, BREAKING THE LAW. ALWAYS PUSHING BOUNDARIES.
RING

HELLO.

IT IS STILL AVAILABLE, AND NO, I DON'T HAVE AN AGENT.

OH MY GOD.

I SOLD MY BOOK.
KIDS! YOUR DAD IS ABOUT TO BECOME A WORLD-FAMOUS PUBLISHED AUTHOR.
I DON'T KNOW ABOUT THAT, BUT IT'S A START.

MY MIND IS RACING WITH ALL THE THINGS I NEED TO DO TO BUILD THIS WRITING CAREER. I'M THINKING ABOUT MARKETING AND SO MANY THINGS RIGHT NOW.
I CAN'T WAIT TO COME TO A BOOK STORE AND HEAR YOU READ A CHAPTER OUT LOUD.
PEOPLE STILL GO TO BOOK-STORES?
THERE'S ONE RIGHT THERE ON 3RD STREET.
I KEEP THINKING ABOUT MY BIRTHDAY SURPRISE. THAT WAS PRETTY WILD.
I HAD A FEELING YOU'D LIKE THAT.
WHAT'S NOT TO LIKE?
I'LL HAVE TO BRING MY A-GAME TO RECIPROCATE THAT.
MY BIRTHDAY IS COMING UP.

DO YOU WANT TO TRY A THREESOME WITH ANOTHER GUY?
THAT SOUNDS FUN. EITHER THAT OR MAYBE WE TRY ONE OF THOSE PUPPY PILES?
I'M LEVELING UP FAST WITH ALL THIS EXPERIENCE, BUT I'M NOT QUITE THERE FOR THE ORGIES YET.
YOU WANT TO DO IT WITH CLINT?
NAH. I THINK WE SHOULD FIND SOMEONE NEW ONLINE IN CASE IT GOES BAD. I'D HATE TO LOSE ONE OF OUR FRIENDS.

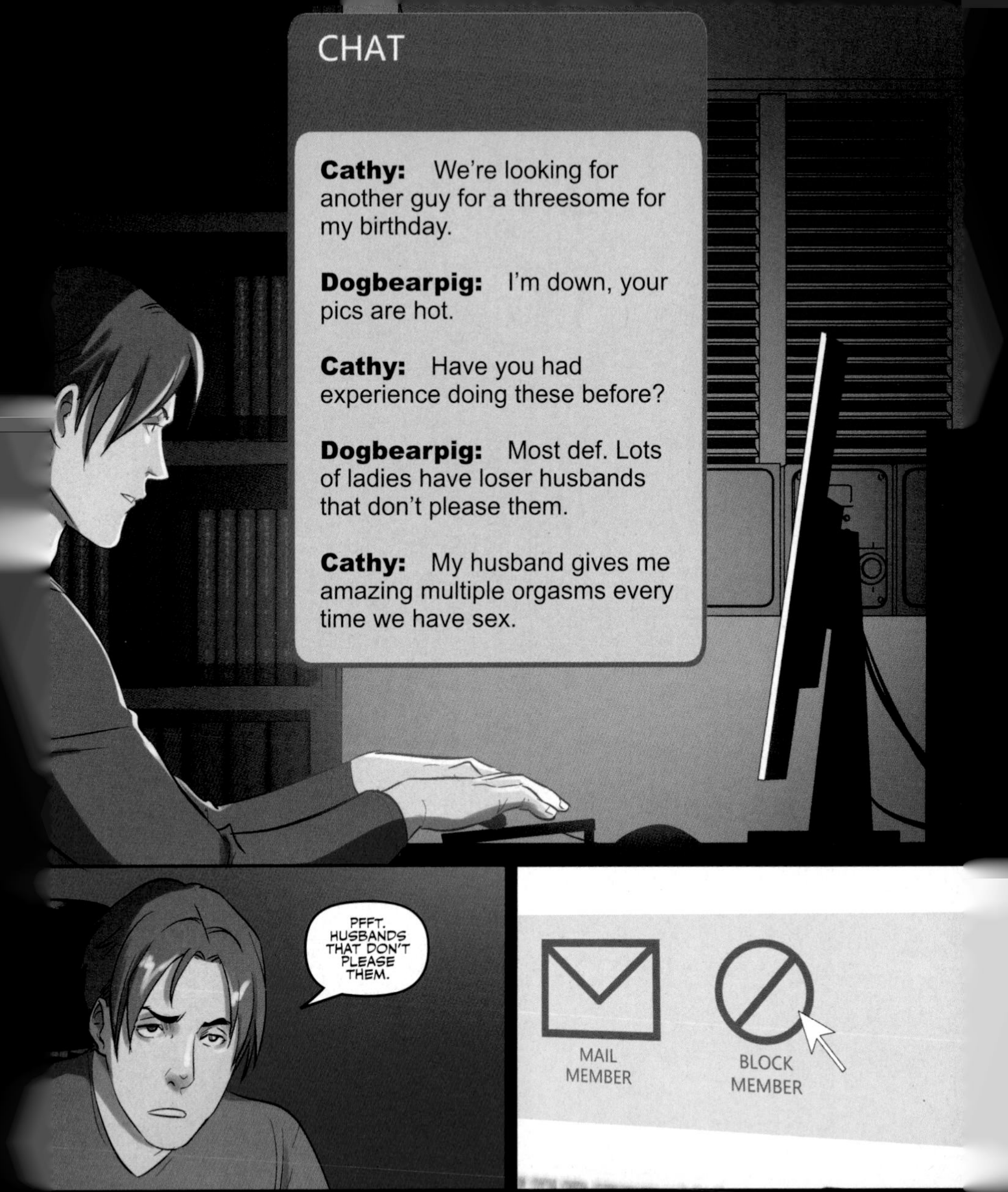

CHAT
Cathy: We're looking for another guy for a threesome for my birthday.
Dogbearpig: I'm down, your pics are hot.
Cathy: Have you had experience doing these before?
Dogbearpig: Most def. Lots of ladies have loser husbands that don't please them.
Cathy: My husband gives me amazing multiple orgasms every time we have sex.
PFFT. HUSBANDS THAT DON'T PLEASE THEM.
MAIL MEMBER
BLOCK MEMBER

Cathy: How many threesomes have you done with married couples?

69warrior: A few, but I can't wear condoms because I'm allergic to latex.

Cathy: That's a dealbreaker, sorry.

Dogbearpig: Your loss, my cock is epic. Like one of those Greek statues.

Cathy: Have you ever seen one of those up close? Their dicks are all small. Yours must be, too.

Lonegunman: I'd definitely be down, you're super-hot.

Cathy: Thanks.

Lonegunman: Would it be okay if I filmed it so I could jerk off to it? I can shoot all over your pretty little face. You'll love it.

Cathy: That will never happen. Do couples let you film them?

Lonegunman: Not that they were aware of.

Nick: To be honest I've not done this before, and it scares me a bit. I just got out of a relationship and thought I'd try this out. I'm trying to focus on school right now so not a lot of time.

Cathy: How old are you?

Nick: I'm twenty-two.

THIS GUY SEEMS NICE, BUT HE'S YOUNG.

YOU WANT TO BE A MILF?

HE'S CUTE. I'M DOWN.

YOU SURE? IT WON'T BE WEIRD DOING A COLLEGE GUY?
HE'S ONLY SIX YEARS YOUNGER THAN ME, THAT'S TWENTY FEWER THAN YOUR DAD AND HIS NEW CHICA.
YOU'RE FIVE YEARS OLDER THAN ME, WHAT'S THE BIG DEAL?
OKAY, LET'S SET UP A VIDEO CHAT ONCE YOU'RE DONE DOWN THERE.

I HOPE THIS GOES SMOOTHLY. WE'VE DONE SO MANY OF THESE FOR DAN, IT ONLY SEEMS FAIR THAT I GET TO TRY IT TOO.
I'M TRYING TO KEEP A SMILE ON MY FACE TO EASE CATHY'S CONCERNS, BUT I *AM* CONCERNED ABOUT THIS.
I DON'T WANT TO BE ONE OF THOSE GUYS THAT WANTS TO HAVE SEX WITH TONS OF WOMEN BUT FLIPS OUT WHEN A GUY TOUCHES HIS WIFE.
I'VE GIVEN IT A LOT OF THOUGHT AND FOR THIS FIRST ONE I THINK I'D PREFER TO JUST WATCH. IF WE'RE GOING TO TRY, LIKE, A DOUBLE PENETRATION OR SOMETHING, I'D RATHER DO THAT WITH SOMEONE I'M A LITTLE MORE COMFORTABLE WITH.
THAT'S FINE WITH ME. I'LL BANG YOUR BRAINS OUT AFTER HE LEAVES.
HEY THERE. SORRY I'M A LITTLE LATE, I'VE BEEN HERE FOR A WHILE. I HAD TO WORK UP THE COURAGE TO COME OVER TO YOU.
AWW, THAT'S CUTE. DON'T WORRY, I WON'T BITE... HARD.
HI, UH, DAN, IT'S NICE TO MEET YOU.
LET'S GET THE PARTY STARTED.
WE'VE NOT DONE THIS BEFORE EITHER, SO RELAX.
WE TALKED ABOUT IT AND I'M JUST GOING TO WATCH.

ARE YOU SURE YOU'RE OKAY WITH THIS?
YEAH, SHE GETS ME OTHER GIRLS ALL THE TIME, SO FAIR'S FAIR.
SHE'S SO PRETTY, YOU'RE A LUCKY MAN.
PEOPLE KEEP TELLING ME THAT.
JUST REMEMBER THE RULES. NO ROUGH STUFF AND DON'T LEAVE ANY MARKS. FOLLOW HER LEAD AND YOU HAVE TO WEAR A CONDOM FOR PENETRATION.
WOW.
YOU OKAY WITH THIS, DAN?

THAT WAS FAST, YOU ABLE TO GO A SECOND TIME?
YEAH, JUST GIVE ME A MINUTE.
HOW YOU DOING OVER HERE, BABE?
I'M GOOD. DON'T WORRY ABOUT ME.
JUST DO YOUR THING AND HAVE FUN. I LOVE YOU.
I LOVE YOU, TOO.

COMPERSION WAS SOMETHING I WASN'T SURE I'D BE ABLE TO FEEL, BUT I GET IT NOW.
IT IS ACTUALLY MAKING ME HAPPY TO WATCH CATHY EXPERIENCE THIS PLEASURE AND JOY.

YOU OKAY?
YEAH.
WAIT! OH MAN...THE CONDOM BROKE.
WHAT THE HELL?! YOU HAD TO HAVE FELT THE DIFFERENCE.
I'M SO SORRY. IT WAS AN ACCIDENT.
GET OUT.

ARE YOU OKAY? I'M NOT MAD.
OH HONEY, I'M SO GLAD TO HEAR YOU SAY THAT.
YOU'LL NEED TO GET AN STD TEST.
YEAH.
IT'S NOT YOUR FAULT.
WE'LL NEED TO CANCEL SOME OF OUR SWINGING PLANS UNTIL YOU GET THE TEST RESULTS BACK.
I'VE NEVER HAD AN STD BEFORE.
JANNIE, THAT GIRL I WAS DATING BEFORE YOU GAVE ME CHLAMYDIA. YOU POP A COUPLE PILLS AND IT'S RESOLVED.

YOU NEVER TOLD ME THAT.
I WAS EMBARRASSED BY IT AND WANTED TO FORGET IT.
I'M FEELING A LITTLE NEEDY RIGHT NOW, WILL YOU SHOWER WITH ME?
HOW CAN I SAY NO TO THIS WOMAN? I LOVE HER SO MUCH.
I'M UPSET, BUT I'M SURE THIS HAS HAPPENED MANY TIMES IN THE SWINGER LIFESTYLE.
HEY, BEAUTIFUL.

THAT THEY DON'T HAVE SAME DAY TEST RESULTS IN TODAY'S DAY AND AGE SURPRISED ME. I'VE HAD TO WAIT A FEW DAYS TO GET THE TEST RESULTS BACK.
DAN HANDLED THIS WHOLE THING SURPRISINGLY WELL.
I KIND OF EXPECTED HIM TO SAY WE'RE DONE WITH SWINGING, BUT THINGS SEEM NORMAL.
THAT MAKES ME HAPPY. THE LAST THING WE NEED NOW IS SEISMIC CHANGE IN OUR RELATIONSHIP.
WE'VE GOT THE TWO WITH FRANK AND HIS CREW. AT FOUR THEY NEED YOU UPSTAIRS FOR A MEETING WITH THE FINANCE GROUP.
I MISS ONLY HAVING TO WORRY ABOUT MARKETING AND SALES. ACCOUNTING, HR...THAT STUFF SUCKS.
AND YOUR DOCTOR CALLED WHILE YOU WERE ON THE PHONE WITH JAPAN, HE SAID HE WAS EMAILING YOU.
AND HERE IT IS.

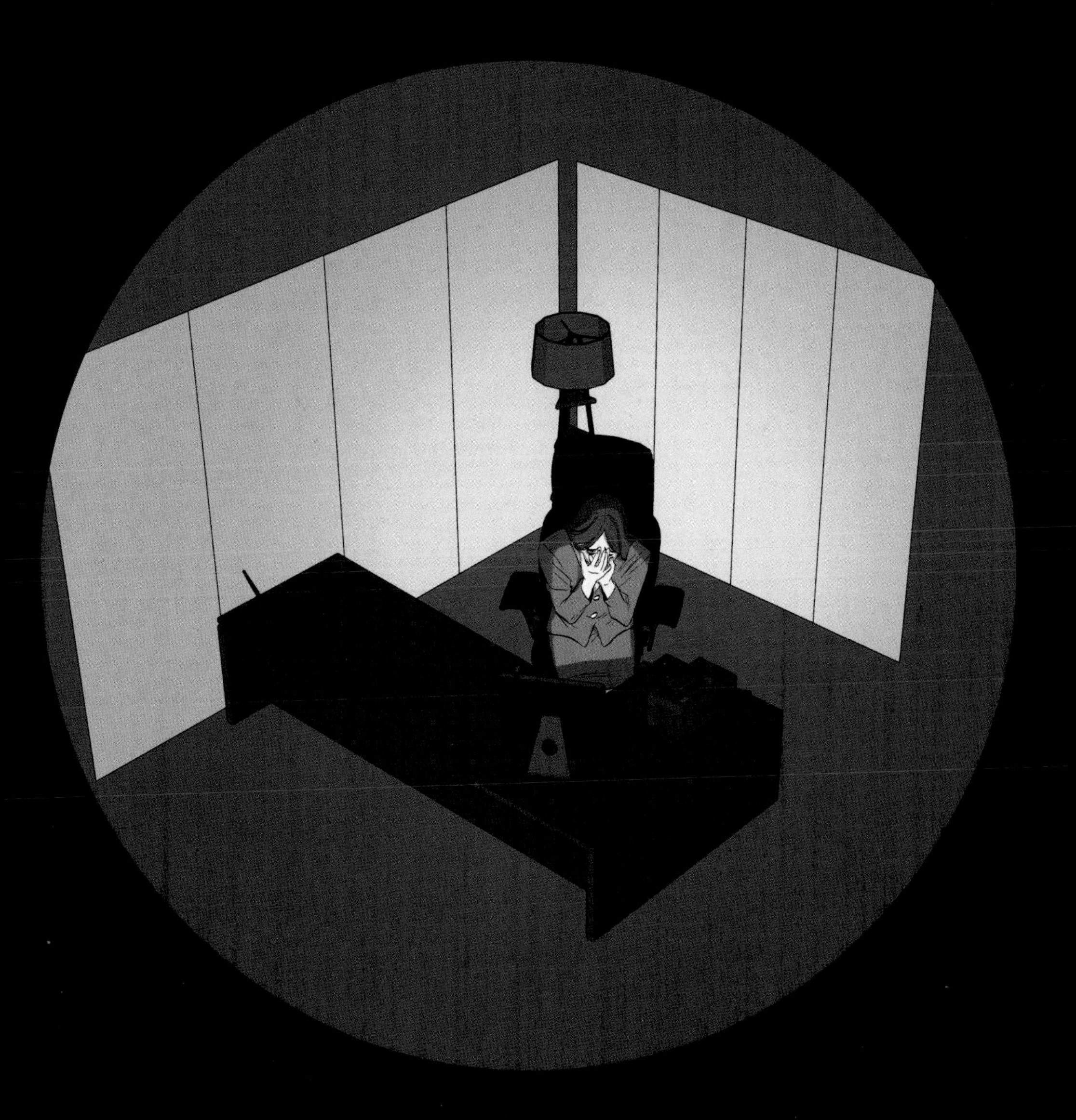

TO BE CONTINUED IN SWING v4!

MATT HAWKINS

is a veteran of the initial Image Comics launch. Matt started his career in comic book publishing in 1993 and has been working with Image as a creator, writer, and executive for over twenty years. President/COO of Top Cow since 1998, Matt has created and written over thirty new franchises for Top Cow and Image including THINK TANK, THE TITHE, STAIRWAY, GOLGOTHA, and APHRODITE IX as well as handling the company's business affairs.

YISHAN LI

is a British/Chinese comic artist currently living in Shanghai. You can see a list of her projects at www.liyishan.com. Yishan Li has been drawing since 1998 and has been published internationally, including USA, France, Germany, Italy, and the UK. She has worked for publishers such as DC and Darkhorse and her last project was *Buffy: the high school years* graphic novels.

LINDA SEJIC

is a digital comics artist specializing in an expressive, dynamicart style. Her first major project with Top Cow was WILDFIRE, written by Matt Hawkins, which showcased her unconventional, character-focused technique and established her as an up-and-coming talent. Her critically acclaimed webcomic BLOODSTAIN is currently published in print from Top Cow, and is on its third volume. Linda lives in Croatia with her husband, illustrator Stjepan Sejic.

SEX ED

Thank you for reading Swing Volume 3! I appreciate you so very much, without you I'd be doing something dramatically different…and I really like what I do. =)

It's September 2020 as I write this, and I am still at home sheltered in place for month number six. Crazy, isn't it? I'm glad that I can vicariously live through the lives of some of my characters as my own life has been quite boring as of late. I hope you are all safe at home with your loved ones with you. Fortunately for me I live with my 18-year-old son who is in his first year of college and that keeps me from being too lonely (well that and my three cats, see below). That my son missed his high school graduation, prom, and so many other things last Spring makes me incredibly sad. We're all dealing with a lot right now, so be sure and self-care. You need to love yourself. You really can't functionally love someone else if you don't care about yourself.

September is an important month for me because it has my birthday in it. This book doesn't come out until late October, so by the time you read this I'll be 51. That age seems old to my 18-year-old self, seems young to me now.

MY CATS
I have two cats I inherited from wife number two and one I got from a shelter. The big darker colored one is Fatty. Jenni named him after the cat from Sex and the City. The tan and black one is Nugget, who is crazy smart and can pee in the toilet (seriously). The last one is Muggs, the black and white with the half Hitler mustache. He's my cat, the only one I got on my own. When my last Corgi died a few years ago I was sad and went to the shelter to get another dog. Muggs was this tiny kitty and he meowed at me. I put my face down by his cage to look at him and he stuck his paw through the bars and tapped me on the cheek with his paw. It was so cute I melted immediately and took him home. Fatty is my son Luke's cat and Nugget, well he's a sneaky, mean, vocal cat so loving him is hard. I've had dogs my entire life. I grew up with a German Shepherd named Alex, who I have a picture somewhere of me riding him when I was like 2. I miss having a dog. They love unconditionally. Cats are a whole different thing. I think it's good for people to have cats because it teaches us how to earn affection (heh). In Swing V4 the family will be getting their first pet. I haven't decided yet if it's a dog or a cat. Open to suggestions!

SUGAR STORY CROSSOVER
In SUGAR the two main characters are Julia Capello and John Markham. John has a douchey friend/business partner named Richard Bryant. That character appears in the Orlando lifestyle club scene talking to Dan and Cathy and he gives me the creeps just writing him. I pitch SUGAR as a modern-day *Pretty Woman*, which ties into the joke I used in this book when Dan's father's fiancé says she doesn't know who Julia Roberts is. I used that line in the book because this happened to me on a date with a younger woman last year. She was asking me about my work and did not know who Julia Roberts was and had never heard of *Pretty Woman*. If memory serves this woman was twenty-nine which is too young for me if you go by the ½ +7 rule. Julia and John from Sugar will both appear in Swing V4.

SUNSTONE/BLOODSTAIN CROSS-OVER VIA MOONSTONE GATE

SWING, SUNSTONE, BLOODSTAIN, and SUGAR all inhabit the same Sejic-verse as I call it. Dan is in an endgame raiding guild for a fictional fantasy video game called Moonstone Gate with Ally from SUNSTONE and Vlad/Elly from BLOODSTAIN. I asked Linda for more detail about the game itself and she wrote this to me:

> *"Ether Elly or Ally are guild leaders.(one is vice the other guild master) Vlad joined up much later and he was inexperienced and they power-leveled him. Elly is in charge of finances in the guild as she is the type of gamer who will just hoard gold and materials but never spend it on anything. Which is kind of ironic…she's rich in-game but poor in real life. Elly used to be a part of a bigger guild before she went working for Vlad. After that she did not play for a few months and was kicked for inactivity. When she returned to the game they decided to make a new guild in an attempt for it to be a more friendlier private experience."*

RULES AND BOUNDARIES FOR SWINGING

These are for every couple and individual to determine for themselves. I've heard these equated to the safe word in S&M but it's not quite the same. Safe word is defined by Merriam Webster as, "a code word or series of code words that are sometimes used in BDSM for a submissive to unambiguously communicate their physical or emotional state to a dominant, typically when approaching, or crossing, a physical, emotional, or moral boundary." Rules and boundaries are hard no's for people. They are fluid because people change them over time as they become more comfortable or desire to try something new. Some people are fine with meeting people separately, or separate rooms, but most swinger couples I've met don't do that. They only "play together". Dan and Cathy's rules were printed in V2 and I'll reprint them here:

Untitled

View Zoom Add Page Insert Text Shape

Rules

1) We only play together, never separately.

2) No exchanging of contact information other than the joint email and messaging app we'll be using.

3) No taking one for the team. Both of us need to be attracted to the other person.

4) No monster cock dudes.

5) Transparency and honesty in all things.

6) Condoms for any penetration (unless it's us, of course).

7) If either of us isn't into it at any point (even mid-sex) we stop and leave and promise not to be mad about it.

8) I'll do the online chatting to vet people, but I'll pretend to be you.

9) The goal is variety, so let's limit the number of times we hook up with the same couple to prevent possible emotional attachment.

10) No individual outside contact of any kind with people we've played with.

We always do our communication together. If this happens by accident (one of us runs into a play partner at the grocery store) we tell the other immediately.

NEGATIVE BOOK REVIEWS SOLELY BECAUSE OF CONTENT

SWING and SUNSTONE have been two of Top Cow's most positively reviewed books of all time. The word of mouth on these books has been amazing, so THANK YOU for spreading the word of the Sejic-verse! It does amuse both myself and the Sejics that there are a small number of reviewers that give these books negative reviews SOLELY based on the fact that they find the content itself morally objectionable. I watched a YouTuber talking about these books and I actually started laughing. The guy was going on and on about how horrible these books are, but then he'd talk about how much he liked certain scenes and that the characters felt "so real". You can't please everyone all the time. If you actually want to hurt my feelings, a review talking about how much you normally love these books, but this one didn't do it for you...that would sting.

HARM AND OFFENSE PRINCIPLES

I'm including this as a philosophical discussion of ethical non-monogamy...and everything for that matter. I believe in the Harm principle, less so in the Offense principle. I don't go out of my way to offend anyone, but if I do and it doesn't harm anyone what's the huge deal? I know there are cases you can argue, but I'm speaking generally.

From Wikipedia, the ***Harm principle*** holds that the actions of individuals should only be limited to prevent harm to other individuals. John Stuart Mill articulated this principle in *On Liberty*, where he argued that *"The only purpose for which power can be rightfully exercised over any member of a civilized community, against his will, is to prevent harm to others."* An equivalent was earlier stated in France's *Declaration of the Rights of Man and of the Citizen of 1789* as, *"Liberty consists in the freedom to do everything which injures no one else; hence the exercise of the natural rights of each man has no limits except those which assure to the other members of the society the enjoyment of the same rights. These limits can only be determined by law."*

The ***Offense principle*** refers to a theory of crime which demands a moral or legal ground for enshrining an actor's behavior. Additionally, the principle supports that offending someone is less serious than harming someone, the penalties imposed should be higher for causing harm.

MISCONCEPTIONS ABOUT SWINGERS

In my research I came across a website called Swingershelp.com that is a good starting point for anyone that might be interested in considering this alternative lifestyle. It had a section called misconceptions about swingers (hence my paragraph title). They did not respond to my email asking permission to reprint some of their content, so maybe next time, but this section raised many things that I think are common misunderstanding or misinterpretation.

FIGHT SCENE

The fight scene in the first part of the book might seem a bit overdramatized, but I based this on actual events, and I reigned it in a bit. Breeching any boundary is a trust issue and it caused Dan and Cathy huge problems because he was already trepidatious about swinging at all. I've seen long time swingers get in a fight over one of them calling another person attractive. I saw a woman scream at a man for him not handing her a drink fast enough. I've come to learn that often fights are more about larger issues that need to be resolved that small instances sometimes bring to the forefront. The article I link below from Psychology Today talks about how small fights start:

> *"The cause of arguments and fights is a lack of mutual, empathic understanding. When empathy is not engaged, then people revert to a self-protective mode and become judgmental. The result is a bad feeling on both sides and no happy ending."*

https://www.psychologytoday.com/us/blog/healing-and-growing/201806/the-number-one-cause-arguments-and-fights

ORAL FROM WOMEN

I never knew this, but I've had a lot of women tell me that they give better oral sex to women than men do. The reasoning is that women know their bodies better and are gentler with it than men are. One woman told me she's bisexual only for this reason. Some people like it rough, some don't, again it's all about preference.

NETWORKING IN LIFESTYLE

One of the things I noticed is that there are a lot of men in their 40s and 50s with younger wives that swing. A lot of these are phenomenally successful people. It's not cheap to be in lifestyle. A single club visit could set you back \$300–\$500 easily. The point is that I've actually made some stellar contacts for business and other things by meeting people in the lifestyle.

LESS DUELING NARRATIVE IN THIS VOLUME

In the first two volumes I used a lot of dueling hers and his narrative captions. I did the same thing in this volume, but to a lesser extent. In the earlier volumes I used it to show the disparity between what the characters were thinking and what they were saying (one of my favorite things to do). It's a good way to illustrate neurosis and fears. There's less of it in this volume BECAUSE they are communicating better.

That's it for this volume! If you liked this book be sure to check out:

Unfortunately I'm not doing a lot of conventions this year since there aren't any, but if you want to chat with me or keep up to date on what I'm doing follow our social media feeds.

Carpe Diem,

Matt Hawkins
Los Angeles, September 2020
Twitter: @topcowmatt | http://www.facebook.com/selfloathingnarcissist

Prologue

The butterfly that started the storm

I SEE BUTTERFLIES.
I REMEMBER SOMETHING SILLY THAT HEURECA TOLD ME... SHE MADE IT SEEM SO IMPORTANT.
"TELL ME IF YOU EVER SEE BUTTERFLIES!"
IT WAS RIDICULOUS, REALLY.
SHE SAID: "IF YOU SEE THE BUTTERFLIES, IT MEANS YOUR BROKEN HEART IS BLEEDING AND YOU WILL LIKELY DIE."

I SAID... I THOUGHT BUTTERFLIES WERE SUPPOSED TO BE IN YOUR STOMACH.
"NO." SHE SAID.
"HEARTBURN COMES FROM YOUR STOMACH, BUTTERFLIES COME FROM YOUR HEART."
IT WAS THE DUMBEST THING I'VE EVER HEARD.
NEVER EVEN OCCURRED TO ME IT COULD BE TRUE.

AS THE DELIRIUM KICKS IN I REMEMBER THAT OTHER THING ABOUT BUTTERFLIES...
THE BUTTERFLY EFFECT— YOU KNOW, WHERE ONE FLAPS ITS WINGS ON ONE SIDE OF THE WORLD AND STARTS A CHAIN REACTION THAT CAUSES A HURRICANE ON THE OTHER SIDE OF THE WORLD.
WELL. HERE I AM DYING AT THE EYE OF THAT HURRICANE...
AND MY LAST THOUGHTS ARE OF THAT BUTTERFLY THAT STARTED IT ALL.

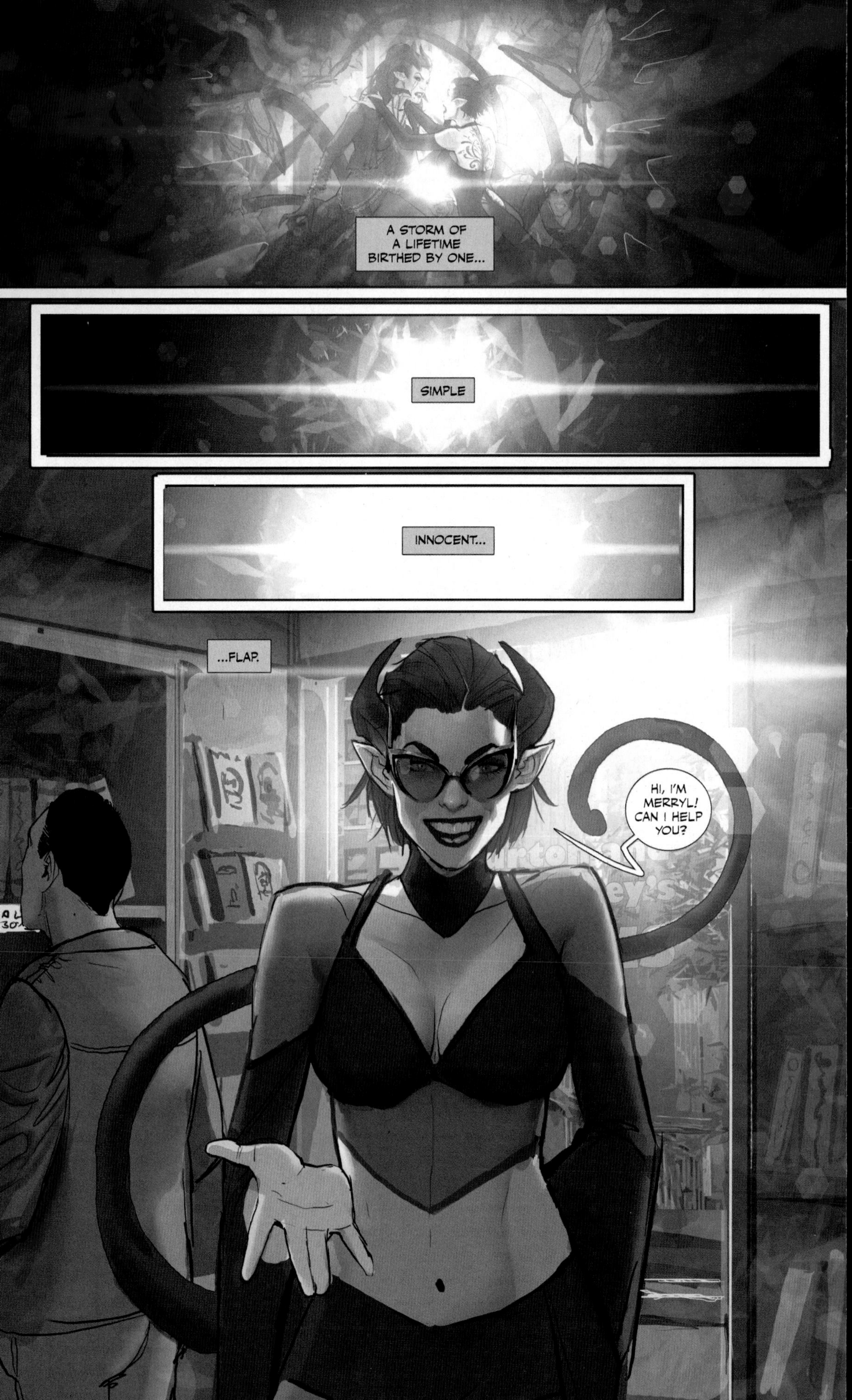
A STORM OF
A LIFETIME
BIRTHED BY ONE...
SIMPLE
INNOCENT...
...FLAP.
HI, I'M
MERRYL!
CAN I HELP
YOU?

YEAH, WE'RE LOOKING FOR MORE BOOKS FROM THIS SERIES, OR IF YOU CAN RECOMMEND SOMETHING SIMILAR, MAYBE?

UH, NO, UNFORTUNATELY. AS FAR AS I KNOW THE AUTHOR IS WORKING ON THE SEQUELS, BUT YOU'LL HAVE TO WAIT.
OH... I SEE...

NOTHING TODAY, THANKS!

MMMHM! HAVE A GOOD ONE!

OH, AND PULL THE DOORS HARD, PLEASE! THE LOCK IS A BIT WEIRD!

MMMMNNNH! WELCOME TO BURTON AND KNIGHTLEY'S BOOKS!
HEH, THANKS, SLOW DAY?
TRY SLOW YEAR!

ANYWAYS, I'M MERRYL, HOW CAN I HELP YOU?

I'M... UH...
RACHEL.
I-- I'M LOOKING FOR SOME FANTASY ARTBOOKS.

YOU OKAY? YOU SEEM KINDA NERVOUS.
Y--EAH... NO. I'M FINE.

WELL, THE ARTBOOKS ARE THAT WHOLE VERTICAL SECTION THERE.

RIGHT... UM, I'LL JUST... I'LL JUST CHECK THEM OUT, THEN.
SURE! LEMME KNOW IF YOU NEED ANY HELP!

RACHEL'S FIRST REACTION TO MERRYL WAS SIMILAR TO MINE.
SOMEONE LOOKS STRANGE IN THE BIG CITY?
SHRUG IT OFF AND MIND YOUR OWN BUSINESS.
LET OTHERS ASK THE QUESTIONS.

HEY, YOU GOT ANY MORE COOK BOOKS?
SURE! ANYTHING SPECIFIC?

THANK YOU, DEAR, YOU'RE AN ANGEL.
AW, THANKS!
...

THEN AGAIN, THERE ARE TIMES WHEN YOU GOTTA DO THE ASKING YOURSELF.

HI, ME AGAIN!
OH, HEY, FOUND ANYTHING INTERESTING?
NOT ON THE BOOKSHELVES.
SORRY?
WELL NO ONE ELSE IS ASKING ABOUT IT, SO I MUST BE THE ONLY PERSON HERE OUT OF THE LOOP...
SO, IS THE STORE DOING SOME KIND OF A BOOK PROMOTION OR SOMETHING?
HERE? NAH. WE CAN'T EVEN ARRANGE SIGNINGS WITH AUTHORS THESE DAYS.
RIGHT... RIGHT...
WHAT'S WITH THE COSPLAY THEN?
THE WHAT?
THE WHOLE HORNS AND TAIL THING?
I THOUGHT THAT WAS LIKE A PROMOTIONAL STUNT FOR A BOOK OR SOMETHING?
MY HORNS AND...
WAIT! YOU CAN SEE THESE?
I MEAN, THEY'RE PRETTY LARGE,
ALSO HOW IS THAT TAIL MOVING LIKE THAT?

RIGHT, HOLD THAT THOUGHT.
OKAY EVERYONE THERE'S AN EMERGENCY AND WE'RE CLOSING EARLY TODAY.
WHAT KIND OF EMERGENCY?
WE FOUND TYPOS IN A DICTIONARY. EVERYBODY OUT!
TUG
TUG
NOT YOU!
ALSO, WHAT ARE YOU DOING, THAT'S NOT SANTA'S BEARD!
THIS... THIS IS A REAL TAIL!!!
YES, AND BEFORE YOU START PULLING ON THEM AS WELL, SO ARE THE HORNS!
CONDUCTOR OF THE ORCESTRA
I...WH...
UH...
WHO ARE YOU?

ME, I'M MERRYL ALARIS. I'M WHAT YOUR PEOPLE WOULD CALL A SUCCUBUS.
YOU'RE SHITTING ME!
YOU'RE AN ACTUAL DEMON!?
CONDUCTOR OF THE ORCESTR
OKAY, I'D REALLY APPRECIATE IT IF YOU DIDN'T CALL ME A DEMON.
IT'S A BIT OF A PET PEEVE, OKAY?
MY KIND IS CALLED CUBI.
SHIT, I'M SORRY, IT'S JUST...
THIS IS ALL KINDS OF SURREAL RIGHT NOW.
LIKE... I'M A FANTASY WRITER, I WRITE ABOUT FANTASY CREATURES, AND THE LAST THING I EXPECTED WHEN I GOT OUT OF THE BED TODAY IS TO SEE ONE IN SOME RANDOM ASS BOOKSTORE!

AAAND NOW I'VE GONE AND CALLED YOU A FANTASY CREATURE...
HAH! CERTAINLY BEATS CALLING ME A DEMON!

ANYHOW, I'M JUST HAPPY THAT SOMEONE FINALLY NOTICED ME...
I MEAN, JEESH... IT'S BEEN OVER A YEAR NOW.

SO, BASICALLY PEOPLE JUST DON'T NOTICE UH... THE WHOLE PACKAGE?

NAH. IT'S ALL HIDDEN BY MY GLAMOUR. TO EVERYONE ELSE I'M JUST A REGULAR GIRL WORKING IN A BOOKSTORE...

BUT THEN THERE ARE THOSE LIKE YOU. RARE, PRECIOUS CLIENTS. THOSE READY TO SEE.

THOSE THAT SHINE BRIGHTLY...
THE ONES THAT ARE WORTHY OF OUR BARGAIN.

AND SPEAKING OF WHICH, I THINK IT'S TIME TO SET UP MY REAL SHOP!

W-WAIT! WORTHY OF A BARGAIN?
LIKE... A TRADE FOR MY SOUL?

NOT A DEMON!
OKAY, YEAH I GET THAT BUT... WELL YOU'RE A SUCCUBUS. I MEAN... EVERY STORY, EVERY RPG GUIDEBOOK SAYS THAT YOUR KIND IS ALL ABOUT SOUL FOR SEX BUSINESS.
CONDUCTOR OF THE ORCESTRA

SO IT'S NOT THAT?
NOPE.

SO WHAT IS IT?
LIKE... I DON'T KNOW TELL ME A LITTLE ABOUT YOURSELF? ABOUT YOUR UM... HOME?
CONDUCTOR OF THE ORCESTRA

WELL I'M A HARD WORKING TRADER AND I HAVE A SMALL BUT COMFORTABLE RENT CONTROLLED APARTMENT FOUR BLOCKS FROM HERE.

OH...

NOT FANTASTIC ENOUGH?
HEH, NOT LIVING UP TO YOUR EXPECTATIONS?
WELL... LET'S FIX THAT, SHALL WE?

LIKE I SAID, I'M A BIT OF A BLUE COLLAR WORKER.
BUT IF YOU WANT GLAMOUR...
IF YOU WANT BLISS AND MAGIC...
WELL I GUESS WE COULD WORK SOMETHING OUT!
Coming Soon

SPECIAL PREVIEW
punderworld
BY LINDA SEJIC

AH...
???
OH NO...
THE HOUSE...
NOT AGAIN...
DARLING WAIT!!
TAP
TAP
TAP

AND I'VE BEEN WAITING FOR CENTURIES TO ASK...

MHPHHH... NO. THAT FEELS LIKE OVERSHARING.

SLAM
HUH?

HEY!! WHERE ARE YOU GOING?
TAP TAP TAP

PERSEPHONE!!! STOP!
TAP TAP

I SAID STOP!!
AH!
RRRUSTLE

....
CRACKLE
UH-OH WHAT DID I STUMBLE INTO HERE?
DARLING!
WAIT!!!
WHERE ARE YOU GOING??
OH WHERE DO YOU THINK I'M GOING???
HERMES IS GONE,
IT'S NOT LIKE I CAN GO ANYWHERE!
SO I'M GOING TO THE LAKE TO RELAX LIKE ALWAYS...
OTHERWISE...
OTHERWISE... I'LL STRANGLE EVERYTHING IN VINES!!

OH...
OK.

DO YOU NEED SOME COMPANY?
NO!!

BUT...

WHAT I NEED... IS TO BE ALONE RIGHT NOW!

CAN'T YOU TRUST ME TO BE ALONE...
FOR JUST 5 CHOES* OF WATER?
*APPROXIMATLY 15 MINUTES OF TIME ON THE WATER-CLOCK.

PLEASE.
ONLY 5 CHOES.

...

SIGH...
OKAY.

TAKE THE TIME YOU NEED BUT DON'T TAKE TOO LONG.
I'LL WAIT INSIDE.
TAP TAP TAP

TAP TAP
GAIA GIVE ME STRENGTH...
WHERE DID I GO WRONG?

....
HEH. THE LAKE.
ZEUS MENTIONED THE LAKE AS WELL.
WAIT.
THE LAKE???
HE PUT A *TRAP* THERE!!
I HAVE TO...
I HAVE TO GET RID OF IT BEFORE SHE GETS THERE!!
B-BUT... I'M SUPPOSED TO...
AAAGHH WHAT SHOULD I DO???
TAP
TAP
TAP

CALM DOWN...
CALM DOWN??
TAP
TAP
TAP
BUT HOW?
WHEN SHE'S RIGHT!
SHE'S RIGHT.
IF HE HAD INTENTIONS TOWARDS ME HE WOULDN'T WAIT SO LONG.
I'M A FOOL, SUCH A FOOL FOR WAITING.
AND THINKING THERE COULD BE SOMETHING BETWEEN US.
I DON'T EVEN KNOW HIS NAME.
OR THE DOMAIN HE BELONGS TO...
OR WHAT GOD HE IS OF.

IF HE IS A GOD AT ALL!!
SIGH...
SNIFF
WHERE??

WHERE IS IT?
WHERE DID HE PUT IT??
AGHHH!!
SPLISH
SPLISH
WHAT DOES IT EVEN LOOK LIKE?

NEIGH!
HUH?

punderworld

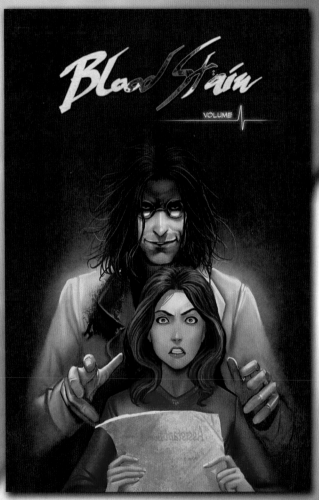

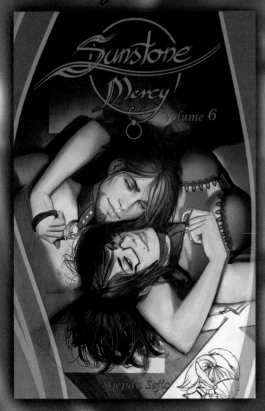

VOLUME 1
DIAMOND CODE:
OCT140613
ISBN: 9781632152121

VOLUME 2
DIAMOND CODE:
FEB150538
ISBN: 9781632152299

VOLUME 3
DIAMOND CODE:
JUN150583
ISBN: 9781632153999

VOLUME 4
DIAMOND CODE:
OCT150579
ISBN: 9781632156099

VOLUME 5
DIAMOND CODE:
MAY160731
ISBN: 9781632157249

The Top Cow essentials checklist:

Aphrodite IX: Rebirth, Volume 1
(ISBN: 978-1-60706-828-0)

Blood Stain, Volume 1
(ISBN: 978-1-63215-544-3)

Bonehead, Volume 1
(ISBN: 978-1-5343-0664-6)

Cyber Force: Awakening, Volume 1
(ISBN: 978-1-5343-0980-7)

The Clock, Volume 1
(ISBN: 978-1-5343-1611-9)

The Darkness: Origins, Volume 1
(ISBN: 978-1-60706-097-0)

Death Vigil, Volume 1
(ISBN: 978-1-63215-278-7)

Dissonance, Volume 1
(ISBN: 978-1-5343-0742-1)

Eclipse, Volume 1
(ISBN: 978-1-5343-0038-5)

Eden's Fall, Volume 1
(ISBN: 978-1-5343-0065-1)

The Freeze, OGN
(ISBN: 978-1-5343-1211-1)

God Complex, Volume 1
(ISBN: 978-1-5343-0657-8)

Infinite Dark, Volume 1
(ISBN: 978-1-5343-1056-8)

Paradox Girl, Volume
(ISBN: 978-1-5343-1220-3

Port of Earth, Volume
(ISBN: 978-1-5343-0646-2

Postal, Volume 1
(ISBN: 978-1-63215-342-5

Stairway Anthology
(ISBN: 978-1-5343-1702-4

Sugar, Volume 1
(ISBN: 978-1-5343-1641-7

Sunstone, Volume 1
(ISBN: 978-1-63215-212-1

Swing, Volume 1
(ISBN: 978-1-5343-0516-8

Symmetry, Volume 1
(ISBN: 978-1-63215-699-0

The Tithe, Volume 1
(ISBN: 978-1-63215-324-1

Think Tank, Volume 1
(ISBN: 978-1-60706-660-6

Vindication, OGN
(ISBN: 978-1-5343-1237-1

Warframe, Volume 1
(ISBN: 978-1-5343-0512-0

Witchblade 2017, Volume
(ISBN: 978-1-5343-0685-1